Raine Cosworth is becoming jaded. One of the top interrogators in the business, he begins to wonder if he's losing what humanity he still possesses. Has he become blind to the suffering he causes, or doesn't he care anymore? His new assignment is to interrogate captured assassin Thorne Wilder. Just another job, right? Until Raine gets a whiff of the man and realizes that Wilder is his mate. What's a harpy shifter to do?

Thorne Wilder is big, black, and beautiful . . . and utterly fearless. He didn't choose to become what he is, but he's not going to cry in his beer about it either. He'll do what it takes to get the job done. And he'll drink anyone's blood with great gusto. So why does the discovery that he has a mate . . . and that mate is none other than the interrogator sent to ferret out his secrets . . . take him aback? All he has to do is grab the shifter and run, right?

Sometimes you have to give up everything in order to gain it all . . .

High Stakes

ISBN: 978-1-4874-3264-5
Cover art by Martine Jardin

Published by eXtasy Books Inc or
Devine Destinies, an imprint of eXtasy Books Inc

Look for us online at:
www.eXtasybooks.com or www.devinedestinies.com

High Stakes
Wildcat Hills Pride 7

By

Liza Kay

DEDICATION

If you do not change direction, you may end up where you are heading.
— Lao Tzu

Chapter One

Raine drummed his fingers on his slack-clad thigh. Shifting his ass on the annoyingly squeaky sofa, he tried not to show his displeasure. His harpy wasn't too thrilled about cushions smelling intrusively like wet dog. On the other hand, his restlessness might have something to do with the constant exhaustion he'd felt since . . . forever.

Raine pinched the bridge of his nose, trying to battle an oncoming headache. He did his best to ignore the two glaring coyote shifters who stood left and right of the living room door. With their similar features, they had to be brothers. Both were buff, had brown eyes, black hair, and deeply tanned skin. One sported a beard and a cool mohawk, while the other was smoothly shaved. The latter kept staring at Armand, who sat beside Raine.

A woman with black hair styled into a cute bob sat opposite them. She'd led them inside and introduced herself as First Enforcer Gillian Heston. Gillian met Raine's gaze with unapologetic curiosity. Of course she'd known about their visit because Xander—Alpha of the Wildcat Hills Pride—had informed Alpha Donavan. Raine didn't fault the woman for being wary of them, though.

"Are you all right?" Armand asked quietly.

Raine shot his boss a smile that had to have been less than convincing, considering Armand's raised eyebrow. "Headache."

A blond human carrying a tray was a welcoming distraction. He had a bright smile on his handsome face. His floppy hair flew around his head, and he wore the weirdest combination of clothes Raine had ever seen—a purple Hawaiian shirt with huge yellow flowers and white skinny jeans.

From the subtle cough beside him, Raine knew Armand was amused. The human had to be London Fishman, Donavan's mate, since he was the only human currently living with the pack.

"Heya. I'm London. And you guys look terribly uncomfortable." London set the tray on the coffee table and placed his hands on his hips. "I told Donny we should get rid of this thing he calls a sofa. The leather and chrome are a right pain in the ass, pun intended. I brought tea, since Xander mentioned you're from France. You drink tea, right? Or is it the Brits who drink tea? Sorry, I must come across as the biggest ignorant hillbilly." He brushed his hair behind his ear. "Would the neck-less guys sitting in the SUV appreciate a cup of tea as well? Or snacks? I'm sure Joseph can fix something really quick. He's a gem."

Raine shot Armand a look.

Armand blinked. "Um . . . tea is fine, Mr. Fishman. And no, my bodyguards will be fine without tea and snacks."

"London, please. I'm trying to teach these old bores to relax and not be so formal." London jerked his thumb over his shoulder at the two men manning the door. "The glowering dude is Cortez Montega, the one with the cool hair is his brother Raul. They're Donny's betas, in case nobody took the time to introduce them. Donny's getting dressed. He'll be with us shortly."

Raine checked his watch, saw that it was nine-thirty. He looked up when London huffed.

"Don't judge, dude." London flicked his hand. "When you meet your mate, you'll understand not wanting to leave your bed. I guess you haven't found her or him yet, or you wouldn't be on this job. I can't imagine spending a day without my Donny. And I know he feels the same." London busied himself pouring tea before focusing on Armand. "I understand you're royalty?"

Armand chuckled as he accepted the cup from London. "Not really. I'm Armand Dubois, the president of the European Shifter Council, ESC for short. At least I am for a couple more months." He gave London one of his typical warm smiles that explained his landslide election results—and the many single men and women vying for his attention.

London whistled. "Awesome. Although I have to be honest, I've never trusted politicians. Sorry." He handed Raine a cup. "They're a bit on the shady side. My grandfather's in local politics and the man hasn't an honest bone in his whole body. Same as my fire-and-brimstone preaching grandma."

Taking the cup, Raine eyed the brew suspiciously. He sniffed it. "What is it?"

"Ylang ylang with lavender."

Armand made a weird choking noise and shot London a forced-looking smile. "Thank you. Sounds lovely."

Raine placed the untouched cup on the coffee table while holding London's gaze. Armand might be the poster boy for diplomacy, but Raine wasn't. He refused to drink something that sounded like an ingredient of laundry detergent.

Some would go as far as calling Raine a bastard. *Like Jules and Romeo.* So what? He was fucking tired of diplomacy and putting up a front. Two years of undercover work in the American Shifter Council, and he barely recognized himself.

I need a vacation. For ten years or so. Raine had tried to uncover illegal activities in the leadership ranks, following reports of several missing shifters who'd moved to the States. Their families back home in Europe had reported their relatives missing when they couldn't contact them. According to Raine's investigation, most of them had been assassinated at President Richard Thoreau's command.

London arched a brow and looked pointedly at Raine's cup. "All right. So you stayed with my Wildcat Hills family for a while? How is everyone? Of course I talk with Viggo and Jax on the phone several times a week, but it's not the same as living with them. We had so much fun! Pulled a ton of pranks. Asa mentioned he needs a spa day, and I'd love to accompany him. We can indulge in some cucumber masks while we get our nails done and gossip about everyone."

"I told you I have no problem with you joining Asa, as long as you take Gillian or Carol with you as protection."

Raine immediately recognized the entering man from the Council file he'd read.

Donavan Haas was much shorter than Raine had thought. London had at least three inches on his alpha mate. Nevertheless, Donavan emitted an air of power that raised the hair on Raine's arms. His harpy moved restlessly inside him, wary about the stronger shifter in the room.

Armand stood and straightened his suit jacket before he offered his hand to Donavan. "Alpha Haas. Thank you for your hospitality. Armand Dubois. I'm pleased to meet you. This is my associate, Raine Cosworth."

Donavan shook his hand and held it for a moment longer, never breaking Armand's gaze, as though he was trying to find something in Armand's eyes. Finally he nodded and motioned for the sofa. "Let's sit and chat. I understand Xander wants you to interrogate our prisoner?" He fixed on Raine. "Associate, hm? Apparently you're exceptionally skilled in the art of retrieving information, Mr. Rainier Rousseau. You see, so am I." Don grinned, showing even white teeth.

Raine suppressed a shudder at Donavan's intense stare. "You know my real name. Congratulations." He lowered his gaze and brushed a piece of lint off his leg.

Up until last year, nothing and nobody could've made him back off a challenge. Whenever Armand needed information, he'd sent Raine to retrieve it. And Raine had been good at his job. Maybe too good, since he'd fucked up so spectacularly with Jonathan Armitage.

The corrupt eagle owl shifter had been Raine's partner during his undercover work at the Council. Raine hadn't eliminated him fast enough, too eager to collect more info from the man. Consequently, he'd risked Jules Armitage's life. Jonathan's younger brother had been undercover as well, working for Alpha Xander. Jonathan had tried to kill his brother for his betrayal.

"Rainier?" Armand asked quietly.

Clearing his throat, Raine rubbed his fingers through his hair. "Raine, please. I'd like to give it a try. I mean"—he noticed Cortez frown heavily—"I'll get it done."

Donavan's eyebrows climbed up his forehead, but he said nothing as he linked his fingers over his knee.

London wasn't as tactful as the alpha. "You *think* you'll get it done? Have you met an assassin before? Do you know how they operate? I had a run-in with them twice, and I almost died." London lifted one hand to his throat. "It *wasn't* funny. Bailey's teeth chomping at my neck is the stuff horror stories are made of. The assassins are even stronger than the average shifter. I bested Thorne Wilder because I had Precious with me."

"Precious?" Raine looked back and forth between the men. "Another enforcer?"

Donavan smirked. "His shotgun."

"A present from my mate," London said, puffing up his chest. "Shot the damn fucker for hurting Donny." He slid his fingers through Donavan's strawberry-blond hair.

Donavan sighed deeply and swatted London's hand away. "I'd like you to stop calling me Donny. It reminds me of the name Donald, and it's . . . disturbing." He shuddered, took a sip of tea, and grimaced. "And what the fuck happened to my coffee?"

"Stop whining." London snatched the cup from his hand and glared. "It's ylang ylang tea. You drink too much coffee anyway. Makes you nervous and jumpy."

Donavan's thunderous look would've made many men cower before him. "Being denied my coffee makes me jumpy. *And* dangerous. Cortez!"

"Right away, sir." The stoic beta peeled his gaze off Armand and vanished. Hopefully to fetch coffee.

Donavan brushed a hand through his hair where London had messed with the tidy strands. He smiled and looped an arm around London's waist when the human perched on the side of the armchair he was sitting on. "Where were we?"

"Wilder." Raine leaned forward, dangling his linked fingers between his knees. "Has he said anything at all? How long has he been in your care?" Thorne Wilder was a former human who'd been experimented on to turn him into an efficient killing machine. The assassin worked exclusively for President Thoreau, who used several teams of altered humans to get rid of his political opponents. Obviously, Donavan Haas had been next on the hit list.

Donavan rubbed London's back. "Two weeks. And nothing from him. We have several deer shifters in our holding cells. They feel nervous around him." He pursed his lips. "I'm not above torturing Wilder for answers since he wanted to kill me. But I can't risk anyone entering his cell. He's too strong. You have to interrogate him without causing physical harm. For the time being."

Armand grunted. "Did you provide blood for him?"

Raine wondered the same. A side effect of the experiments Wilder had undergone was a defect in his metabolism. The assassin's body didn't produce enough blood cells, so Thorne was dependent on another source. Raine had learned from Bailey—a former assassin who worked for Xander—that all assassins drank blood to survive.

Scientifically created vampires. Great.

"How?" Donavan laughed without humor. "I don't have blood reserves lying around. Surprisingly, nobody has volunteered to become his nutrient source." His expression was pure ice.

Raine pulled his cell from his jacket. "I'll text Bailey. He drinks from bags." He typed a quick message. Starved prisoners tended to cooperate when presented with the prospect of food. "I'd like to see the prisoner, please. Get a first impression before we start tomorrow."

"Why not start questioning him right away?" Don asked.

Raine stood and pocketed his phone. "I want him to wonder who I am for at least a night. I will take a look at him, say nothing, and leave." He shrugged as he buttoned his jacket. "Just one of the techniques that have worked for me over the years." At least it had worked on people who hadn't gone through military training and a brutal assassin boot camp. But it was worth a shot.

"Fine with me." Don stood as well. "Raul, Gillian." He briskly took the lead, the beta and enforcer following him. When Raine made to follow them, Armand touched his sleeve.

"I'll wait here. I'm not cut out for . . ." Armand waved his hand.

Raine nodded curtly. Of course he wasn't. He'd brought Raine to do what nobody else had the guts to do. "Yes, sir."

Raine followed Gillian, shivering when he stepped onto the porch and the chilly air hit him full force. Too damn windy for his taste. His harpy wasn't fond of storms either, since they ruffled their feathers. Raine wrapped his arms around himself, wondering how Gillian, dressed in a skin-tight black uniform that looked rather thin, didn't shiver her ass off.

Walking past cute houses and a construction site, Raine

caught sight of other men and women dressed the same way as Gillian and figured they had to be Donavan's fighters.

Gillian nodded to a couple of men dressed in worn jeans and thick flannel shirts who were leaning against a fence. Donavan's pack maintained a steady income from raising beef cattle. As a city boy, Raine had never been on a farm or ranch. Didn't diminish his weakness for tall, buff men in casual clothes.

His gaze lingered on the two cowboys. One of them winked at him. The man turned, hooked his thumb through his belt loop and cocked his hip to one side. The move lured Raine's attention to the heavy bulge in the man's pants.

Raine startled when Gillian grabbed his arm.

She smirked. "Come on, Casanova. You're free to enjoy the amenities of the ranch *after* you've met Wilder." She gave him a knowing once-over. "You won't have trouble finding companionship among our men. Those who work the farm seldom leave pack land, so a visitor is always exciting."

Shaking his head, Raine let her lead him to a building that attracted attention, constructed of solid brick instead of wood. "Not sure if I'm in the right mood to hook up during our stay." Although he was overdue for some action that didn't involve a money exchange. Undercover work sucked, and not in a pleasant way.

Pushing thoughts about his dismal sex life from his mind, Raine brushed past Raul, who once again took post beside the door. He took in the big room they'd entered. In the middle was a large wooden table where three men sat. He assumed they were guards. Cards lay on the table among glasses and bowls filled with snacks. On the left wall was a kitchenette, while a row of desks and monitors adorned the right side.

"This is the main room." Gillian pointed to a door opposite the entrance. "Through there are chambers where the guards can take a short nap as long as someone always mans the monitors, as well as a bathroom. It's also the access to the stairs leading down to the cells." She nodded to the men at the table. "Roy, Carl, and Jerome. We always have three men on duty for six-hour shifts. We had two when we took in the captured deer shifters, but since Wilder joined us, we upped the security."

Raine nodded. "Five deer shifters, right?" Alpha Xander's problems with the Council had started when he'd come across a deer shifter alpha who captured shifters and sold them to Thoreau's research laboratory. Although Hector was on the lam, his men had been arrested and stored on pack lands.

Donavan nodded. "Yes, but one of them stays at my house. Hugh was very helpful. He had nothing to do with Alpha Hector's crimes. He was a victim himself."

Raul grunted quietly.

When Raine turned, he noticed the man's murderous glare. Focusing on Donavan, Raine raised his eyebrow.

"Hugh was attacked by one of Hector's men." Don growled. "Raul rescued him."

Raine guessed there had to be more than mere friendship between the men, but kept his mouth shut. "You have video surveillance in the cells?" He walked over to the row of monitors. Each offered a live-feed for a cell. Two men were lying on their beds. One was doing push-ups in the middle of his cell, while another sat at a table reading a book. The fifth video feed showed a room lacking furniture, save for a nest of blankets in a corner. And it was empty.

"Care to explain this?" Raine pointed at the screen.

Donavan walked up beside him. "Wilder's cell. He used the furniture to build weapons and tools. Tried to open the lock with a tool made from nails, a chair leg, and other stuff he found in his cell. We finally had to take the metal bed frame as well. See this?" He placed his finger on the monitor, indicating the left of the cell. "Behind this wall is a shower and a toilet. The other prisoners can leave their cells to use the community bathroom downstairs one at a time. We can't afford to give Wilder the same courtesy. We built him this and stunned him for the transfer. Nobody wants to see how the guy beats off under the spray or takes a dump, so the camera gives him privacy for that."

Raine pursed his lips. "And there's no way for him to escape while he's out of sight?"

"Not unless he learned to shift into a fish and flush himself down the loo." Don smirked. "Never touch the bars of his cell, by the way."

"Active?"

"Yes," Gillian said behind him. "He once reached through the bars while Roy brought him food and got a hold of the boy's hair. If Jerome hadn't been with him, Wilder would've broken his neck." She met Raine's gaze. "He's a stone-cold killer through and through. The dead expression in his black eyes sends a shiver down my back. And his silence makes everyone nervous."

Raine licked his lips. "What do you expect from me? I gain the best results when I'm actually able to touch the suspect." He glanced at the monitor, then focused on Alpha Haas.

Don cleared his throat. "For now, you're limited to a verbal approach. If that doesn't work . . ."

"Stun guns." Gillian lifted one then pushed it into a holster strapped to her thigh. "Specifically designed for shifters, since we have a higher resistance. Thankfully, Wilder isn't immune to them."

Raine rubbed his eyes with his thumb and index finger. And here he'd thought he'd get this assignment over with and be relaxing on a warm beach by the end of the week. Suddenly he felt bone tired. "In my experience, broken fingers and smashed kneecaps loosen a tongue much faster than verbal threats. I'm not looking forward to wasting the next couple of weeks in a dingy prison negotiating with a tight-lipped vamp."

Gillian snorted. "You're a delight. Beta Alan warned us about your sunny disposition."

"Yes, well, enough chitchat. It's time I met the delightful man."

Gillian snapped her fingers at the men around the table. Jerome rose, and together the three left the main room.

Jerome opened a steel door at the end of the hallway by pressing a series of numbers on a touch pad beside the door.

Raine memorized them just in case. He bet there was another touch pad on the other side of the door to leave the downstairs prison. He didn't want to be trapped with a crazed, blood-thirsty killer if things went wrong.

Gillian smirked. "The code to leave the basement is *not* the same, Mr. Cosworth. But nice try."

Underestimated her. Raine descended the brightly lit stairs between Jerome and Gillian. The basement wasn't the rank, dirty place he'd imagined. The bare concrete walls had been painted white and were blindingly clean. A lemony fresh scent tickled his nose. He didn't see a speck of dust. No webs or spiders, either.

Good. I hate the little eight-legged monsters. Eight arms against two isn't fair.

"Looks new," he mused. "Clean." Raine noticed there wasn't anyone manning the basement. The surveillance was exclusively done from upstairs. He made a note to inform Donavan about his concerns regarding the hole in security. The space at the foot of the stairs provided enough room for a table and a chair or two for more guards.

"It is," Gillian answered. "We gave the place a once-over after Xander caught Hector's men. Don said the cats didn't have a secure enough prison, and we didn't mind lending a hand. The building was built by Donavan's grandfather. He was known to engage in petty squabbles with neighboring packs and needed a place to house prisoners until the other pack paid their ransom."

Raine grunted. Although it was clean, the place still had a weird Hannibal Lecter vibe with its neat row of cells and the hall leading past them. At least it was brightly lit. "Let me guess, Wilder's in the farthest cell?"

"Yep." Gillian popped the *p* and shrugged one shoulder while she put one hand on the butt of the stun gun. "As I said, his silent sulking makes everyone nervous. The deer shifters aren't shy and tend to be quite talkative. Aside from Tobin the Asswipe, they're good little boys."

Raine cocked his head. "What will happen with them? You can't keep them in Pumpkin Creek forever."

Gillian sighed. "They need to be prosecuted for their crimes. But with half the Council in Thoreau's pocket, they'd probably be free in mere minutes." She assessed him with hard eyes. "These guys aren't petty criminals. We're talking shifter trafficking. Do you want me to come with you, or do you think it's better if he meets you alone?"

Raine smiled. "I'd appreciate it if you came with me, but please keep to the background. Jerome should stay behind." He schooled his expression and tugged at his suit jacket, then started down the corridor, his dress shoes clicking on the bare concrete floor.

While he passed the cells, he avoided looking at the inmates. He wasn't here for them. His target was Wilder. The ridiculous thought that the last cell ought to have a huge pane of glass with breathing holes in it produced a chuckle.

The quick bout of humor deserted him when his attention was caught by a set of black eyes. The annoying lemon scent hanging in the air gave way to the utterly delicious aroma of dark chocolate and red wine.

Tension coiled in Raine's belly. Need unlike anything he'd

ever felt hit him like a semi.

Thorne Wilder was six foot five of tightly packed muscles under delicious mocha skin. He was bald—probably naturally so, since he had a beard. Raine doubted anyone had given the guy a razor to shave his head.

Wilder wore gray sweats and a white wifebeater. The clingy fabric made love to his godly upper body. Tattoo sleeves covered his strong arms all the way up to his neck and one side of his smooth head. Long, strong fingers rested on his hips. And although Wilder had to be starving and frustrated after two weeks in a windowless cell, he was the cockiest damn prisoner Raine had ever seen.

His lips . . . Not a grin or a smirk, but the slight curl to his mouth made him look . . . triumphant?

Raine took a deep breath of that wine-and-chocolate scent. Eyes widening in horrified realization, he locked his knees to keep himself from turning and running. Hell, he had the sudden urge to leave Nebraska, maybe buy a plane ticket and return to France.

If he thought he'd fucked up bad on his last job, this one had the potential to turn into an utter disaster. Because Thorne *fucking* Wilder . . . was his mate.

Chapter Two

Eighty-five. Eighty-six. Eighty-seven.

Counting his push-ups should've kept Thorne focused. He'd never before failed to concentrate on the task at hand. His sudden struggle disturbed him. Even hungry as he was, the need for blood like a knife slicing through his belly, he'd been able to plot and plan his escape. Until . . .

Ninety-five. Ninety-six.

Until yesterday.

It was that damn scent. He hadn't been able to enjoy it for long, since one of the guards had mopped the floors after breakfast with the awful lemony crap they called cleaner. But the smell was ingrained in Thorne's brain. To the hungry beast living inside him, the guards and the deer shifters in the other cells smelled good enough to snack on after two weeks of starvation. Still, Thorne had never been more tempted to break through the bars and sink his teeth into a fresh vein than yesterday.

One hundred.

Panting, Thorne rolled onto his back on the floor, relishing the chilliness of the concrete seeping through his skin. He raised his hands and brushed his fingers over his bald head.

Fuck the damn nameless suit. The man hadn't said a word, had only stood and stared at Thorne. He'd probably meant to look intimidating in his posh threads and polished leather shoes that screamed Italian designer, but the fear and horror flickering in his eyes for a split second had fucked up his cool façade pretty good.

The predator in Thorne had loved sensing the man's fear, had immediately latched onto the knowledge and plotted ways to exploit it.

But another, more primal part had flared to life. It was the feeling of an unfinished hunt he'd only felt lurking at the back of his consciousness ever since he'd become a monster.

Thorne had wanted to hunt the man down and tug him against his chest. It had been so many years since Thorne had had the urge to wrap himself around another and hold on tight that the feeling had shocked him.

Thorne closed his eyes, blocking his view of the naked concrete ceiling. Even now his prick twitched for the prettiest set of light blue eyes he'd seen in years. Experiencing arousal after a decade of . . . nothing . . . was a weird sensation. Not unpleasant, but still a surprise.

He took deep breaths, slowing his pulse and forcing his body to relax. His current weakness due to constant hunger made that easier, but he wasn't made to sit on his ass for hours on end. The first couple of days after the relocation to his current cell he'd considered touching the bars just to shake up the monotony of his stay. Thorne doubted the electric shock would be strong enough to kill him, since the coyotes wanted his cooperation. That wouldn't be any worse than what Doc Taylor and the instructors had put him through.

Thorne smirked as he pulled up another image of the stranger. He was tall, but not as tall as Thorne. The dark blue suit clung to his muscled frame. A nifty vest in the same dark blue accentuated a slim waist. And the man's silky black hair, fashionably brushed back, fell to his collar—the perfect length to grab during a feeding.

Thorne had seen men like him before. The stranger was a spiffy, proper Council investigator package that Thorne longed to slice out of his suit and . . .

He moaned quietly and gave his semi a quick squeeze

through the sweats. Fuck, it felt good to need again.

Chuckling quietly, he opened his eyes as he slid his hand under the waistband and fisted his prick. With his free hand he flipped the bird toward the camera in the corner under the ceiling. He wasn't shy. Not since living as a lab rat for so many years. If his jailors wanted to watch his first wank in forever, he didn't give a fuck.

Thorne thought about the dirty things he wanted to do to the stranger if he managed to lure him into his cell. Thorne would turn him, push him up against the wall, and lick a slow, long line up the tempting pale flesh of his neck. He wondered if the man tasted as good as he smelled. Thorne sped up his strokes as his cock flagged a little.

Fuck. No.

Tipping back his head, he imagined sinking his teeth through the man's skin, but that didn't have the desired effect.

Thorne cupped his balls as he remembered the man's crystal-clear blue eyes and the gentle curve of his pale pink lips. When he wondered what those lips would taste like, his balls pulled tight and pre-cum leaked from his slit.

Fuck, yeah. That's more like it.

Thorne would start with the guy's mouth and nibble his way down his body, biting and sucking as he went, leaving dark bruises.

Marks of ownership.

Pushing that troubling thought away, Thorne arched his back and came all over his naked chest. He slowed his hand to a lazy stroking motion, coaxing the pleasure through his body as he tried to prolong the sensation. Thorne laughed freely, amazed how much he'd enjoyed the simple jerk-off session.

The metallic clank of the basement door lock disengaging yanked him from his happy place.

Fucking guards.

Was it time for another round of unsatisfying food? It

wasn't bad per se, but since his body lacked blood, everything had started to taste like cardboard.

Unashamed of the seed caked to his chest, Thorne rolled to his feet. He stuffed himself back into his pants and stretched his arms over his head. He sauntered closer to the bars and sniffed, grunting when his nose picked up the scent of freshly mown grass. Shockingly, his cock twitched in his sweats with renewed interest.

Calm down, boy.

A second later, the stranger appeared on the other side of the bars. Today he wore a gray suit over a red silky looking shirt.

Fucking red.

Had he purposefully tried to make himself look like a snack? If so, he'd succeeded with flying colors. The deep red of the shirt, blood red, accentuated the paleness of the man's smooth skin. His cheeks were . . . flushed.

The man's blue eyes widened as he raked his gaze up and down Thorne's body and focused on his splattered chest. His mouth dropped open and his nostrils flared. Something flashed in his eyes.

Thorne chuckled. "Cat got your tongue?" Never mind that he hadn't said a word since *moving in* two weeks ago. This guy was interesting enough—at least to his usually uninterested dick—to break his silence. "Never seen a guy come all over himself, Red?" Something occurred to him. "Oh, you've been upstairs and watched on the monitors, right? A pervert *and* a stalker." He picked up his shirt from the blankets on the floor. Rubbing it over his chest, he focused on the man. "Did you enjoy the show?"

The stranger licked his lips, black lashes fluttering as he blinked rapidly. He cleared his throat and sidestepped. There was noticeable action in his pants. "Wilder—"

"That's my name. What's yours, Mr. Council Investigator?" Thorne studied the man's reaction. He had an interesting French accent but was trying to suppress it. When his eyes widened, Thorne smirked.

"I'm not with the Council."

Stalking closer to the bars, Thorne sniffed exaggeratingly. His gums tingled, and he knew his eyes must've changed, because his vision had switched slightly. Thorne was more aware of the vein pulsing in Red's neck. "You mean you're not with the *American* Council." The bobbing of the man's Adam's apple confirmed his suspicion. "Europe then, based on your accent. Dubois' lap dog?" He laughed sharply.

Red curled his hands but remained otherwise unresponsive.

Thorne wasn't as dumb as his bosses thought. Being a soldier following orders didn't mean he had no brain. Over the past ten years, he'd made use of his superior's database and learned as much as possible about the big players in the shifter world.

On the surface, Armand Dubois' reputation was as clean as a nun's sheet. Still, he *was* a politician, so of course he had someone do his dirty work. If that someone was Red, he'd clearly been on the job far too long. He showed obvious signs of a bone-deep fatigue. Thorne recognized the signs, because he'd seen them in himself lately.

"I'm Raine Cosworth." He slid his hands into his pants pockets and leaned his back against the wall.

"Good. Tell me your real name or this conversation is over."

Raine laughed and shrugged one shoulder. "Rainier Rousseau."

Now that name sounded like sex on a hot summer day. "Rainier Rousseau," Thorne repeated slowly, a growl in his voice, loving how Raine's pupils widened in reaction. "Nice to meet you. Took you long enough. Honestly, I expected one of the other Councils to step in way sooner. Do you consider yourself a good little agent?" Thorne loved the flush spreading over Raine's cheeks. He loved that he flustered the man so easily.

"You want to talk about me?" Raine arched one perfectly shaped black eyebrow. "I'm flattered, considering you didn't say a word to the coyotes. Don't we all want to feel special?" His tone dripped with sarcasm.

Thorne laughed. "Convince the doggies to let you enter my cell and I'll show you how special I can make you feel, Red."

Raine coughed. "Thanks for the generous offer, but I'm not your pincushion, bloodsucker." He pursed his lips. "By the way, I asked for blood bags to be delivered for you. We don't want you to starve while you're in our care." His smile was sweet as saccharine and absolutely fake.

"Trying to booze me up and take advantage of my sated state, huh? Men, I swear." He winked. "You're all the same. I'd rather you try to talk your way into my pants. Tell me something about yourself and I'll make it worth your while." Thorne needed insight if he wanted to use Raine for his escape. He was damn good at exploiting people's weaknesses. All he had to do was find Raine's. Plus he seriously enjoyed riling the guy after two painfully dull weeks of half-hearted interrogation attempts.

Raine crossed his arms over his chest. "I'm not that interesting. And I'm not here to play your games."

"Oh? I call bullshit." Thorne stepped as close as the bars allowed. "A game is the only thing you're interested in, right? But you thought you'd be the one in charge of it. The one winning it. Good luck with that." He lowered his voice. "Play by my rules or return to Daddy Armand and tell him you crashed and burned."

Something flickered in Raine's eyes.

Gotcha. Is he afraid of failing? "I'm sure he won't mind too much, right? Because you've always been a reliable agent. No harm in fucking up one tiny assignment, is there?" Thorne turned and stalked back to his nest of blankets, sat with his back to the wall, as though he didn't care one way or another about Raine's decision. He closed his eyes and tipped his head back.

"When I return, we can talk about your fucked-up assignment. You lost one man, and the others fled without trying to help you."

When Thorne heard the sound of expensive dress shoes on bare concrete, he smirked but didn't open his eyes.

The other prisoners were given books to entertain themselves. He'd heard them talk about the stories they read. A true prison book club. Thorne hadn't been granted the same courtesy, but he didn't mind too much. He loved to read, but he could just as well occupy his mind with more important things.

Raine was right. The team *had* left him to die. Standard procedure. And it wasn't *his* team anyway. He'd filled in after he'd killed the old commander during an argument, so he didn't expect any loyalty from his men.

Thorne's escape plan was set. He was free to daydream about his plans for Rainier Rousseau. Red would be back soon. Not necessarily because he wanted to, but because he was hell-bent on winning.

CHAPTER THREE

Raine paced the guest room like a caged animal. A quick glance at the clock told him he'd been at it for an hour. Five in the morning. He'd tossed and turned before falling into a disturbing dream he'd woken from with a harsh gasp, clutching his chest like a heroine in a cheesy movie.

Thorne Wilder had starred in a dream so dark Raine had woken with cum caked to his belly and chest.

Dragging his fingers through his hair, he took a deep breath and tried to calm down. Dreams didn't mean a thing. They were just a weird product of his sleep-deprived brain. Had to be burn-out or something. Nothing more. He shuddered at the memory of a set of sharp white fangs.

Kicking the pile of his clothes where he'd left them on the floor before going to bed, he cursed quietly. Just yesterday he'd thought all he needed was a vacation and a good fuck to reclaim his sobriety. Suddenly he found himself in the biggest dilemma in the history of dilemmas.

Armand expected Raine to torture Thorne Wilder if he remained uncooperative. And that might kill the last decent part of Raine's personality. He'd done some fucked-up shit over the years in the name of the greater good, but he'd never go as far as laying a hand on his own damn mate.

Thorne Wilder was their enemy, his loyalty belonging to Thoreau and Taylor, who'd experimented on Thorne. He was a stone-cold killer who'd probably tear out Raine's throat if given the opportunity. But he was Raine's, and the moment Raine had scented him, the guy's many misdeeds ceased to matter. He'd sooner cut off his own arm than cause Thorne as much as a paper cut. But would he be able to reason with the assassin? Convince him that Raine wanted to help him?

"I'm fucked. Hard. Without lube."

He needed fresh air.

Raine stalked to his suitcase and retrieved a gray sweater that he yanked over his head. He slid his legs into his sweatpants, forgoing underwear, as was shifter custom. Not bothering with shoes or socks, he quietly opened the door to his room and peeked into the hallway.

This being a farm, he expected people to be up early, bright-eyed and bushy-tailed, but the alpha's house was surprisingly quiet. Maybe because the business part wasn't in Donavan's hands but managed by Orin Fairbanks, a big and broad veterinarian with a friendly smile and weird sense of humor.

Raine closed the door quietly behind him and padded down the hall to the stairs. He descended and skipped the second to last step because he remembered it had squeaked when he'd hurried up to his room after dinner. He stalked through the empty kitchen, opened the back door, and stepped onto the porch.

He shivered when the cold seeped through the naked soles of his feet. That was exactly what he needed to focus on something other than his current predicament. Raine took a deep breath and let it out slowly through his lips, following the white puff with his gaze until it dissolved. If only his problems could dissolve as easily.

The scent of dirt and animals hung heavy in the air. And . . . coffee?

"Hi."

Raine would forever deny he had done so, but he jumped at the quiet voice that came from the direction of the porch swing and whirled around. Then he groaned.

God, he was so on edge he'd flipped out over a tiny guy in a puffy green jacket whose spindly thin legs ended in a pair of brown Ugg boots. Considering the long black braid that hung over his shoulder all the way to his thighs, his deep tan and dark brown eyes, Raine guessed he was Native American.

"Uh . . . hi." Raine sniffed. "You have to be Hugh."

"Do I?" The guy smiled and lifted a cup to his lips. "Okay. If you say so."

Raine laughed. "Little smartass, huh? Can I sit?" He pointed at the empty seat beside Hugh.

"Suit yourself. There's coffee in the kitchen." He dipped his head toward the door. "I'm always up early and start the first pot. The others won't be up until seven. I enjoy sitting on the porch and watching the farm wake up. Too bad it's so cold. A couple of months ago, the men walked around in nothing but tight jeans and short-sleeved shirts."

Raine sat beside Hugh, careful not to rock the swing too much, and let his gaze wander. Though it was still dark, several men and women were up and about, pushing wheelbarrows or carrying stuff Raine couldn't name. In the distance, he heard the soft sounds of cattle mooing. A peaceful scene. "I understand why you like sitting on the porch, eye-candy aside."

"You had a bad dream."

Raine focused on Hugh. "Excuse me?"

Hugh rolled his eyes. "I have them every night. Don't try to deny it. I won't tell anyone. I'm good at keeping secrets."

Shaking his head, Raine concentrated on a man slowly walking by the porch.

That was the cowboy who'd leered at him yesterday. He lifted one hand to the brim of his cowboy hat and smirked, his dark brown eyes glittering with mischief.

Twenty-four hours ago, Raine would've taken him up on

his blatant offer.

"Be careful with Miles. He's a manwhore."

Raine turned his head and took in Hugh's flushed cheeks. "Talking from experience?"

"He's come on to me a couple of times." A grin split Hugh's face. "Until Raul had a word with him. Raul's my hero." He tugged at the end of his long braid, the flush on his face darkening.

"I met him. He's got a serious glare." Raine laughed. "No wonder Miles keeps his distance. Although Cortez's glare is worse."

Hugh pursed his lips. "Cortez eats duty and sobriety for breakfast. Very intense guy. Don't let him intimidate you."

Raine chuckled. "Don't worry about me. Do you know why I'm in Pumpkin Creek?"

Hugh nodded and took another sip of his coffee. He leaned back and tugged his booted feet onto the edge of the swing. "You're the interrogator. Rumor has it you always get your answers and that you use any means necessary." He glanced at Raine, his gaze surprisingly free of judgment. "Is it true?"

"That I torture people for a living? Sometimes, yes." Raine placed his elbows on his knees and let his hands dangle between his legs. "You don't look shocked. Or disgusted."

"I lived with my uncle for too many years. I've seen . . . things. I experienced things, too." Hugh shrugged. "What you do . . . does it serve a good purpose?"

Raine let his gaze roam and took a deep breath. The distinctive scent of coming snow tickled his nose. "Most of the time? I hope it does," he whispered. "I was sure of it in the past. These days, I wonder."

"You're unexpectedly honest about your sordid job. You're . . . different." Hugh laughed. "I'm used to men trivializing the bad things they've done. Guess you're one of those who beat themselves up over what they do out of duty."

"I'm not a soldier. I'm a spy and an undercover agent who sacrifices people when it's necessary." And he was damn tired of his job. Maybe he should quit, grab Thorne, and vanish.

Hugh placed a small hand on his back. "The prisoner is one, though."

"What?" Raine didn't shrug Hugh's hand off. It had been too long since he'd been touched with no other intention than friendliness.

"Wilder. He's a soldier. I recognized his tattoos. There has to be a sliver of honor left in his body."

Raine bit his lip. "He *was* a soldier. Decided to become an assassin to save his life."

"Understandable." Hugh took a deep breath and pushed from the swing. Their gazes met. "What would you do to save your life?" He dipped his head and vanished back inside, his Ugg boots shuffling over the wooden porch.

Raine sighed deeply.

What would I do to save my life?

He'd never thought about that question in all his years working a dangerous job. Raine had never been worried about his own demise, since he'd resigned himself to the possibility of a violent death.

But what would I do to save someone else's life? What am I willing to sacrifice for my mate's life?

An hour later found Raine sitting on a hard metal chair in the hall in front of Thorne's cell, an open file resting on his knees. He lazily leafed through it, staring at the meager facts they had on his mate. He'd long since memorized them.

Thorne sat cross-legged in his nest of blankets, a paper cup in his hand. Paper, because Donavan had forbidden anything that might be used as a weapon. Thorne hadn't even gotten a straw. Apparently plastic straws were lethal weapons in the hands of former Navy Seals.

Humming, Thorne lifted the cup to his lips. The working of his throat muscles pulled Raine's concentration from the file and to the object of his desire. When Thorne lowered the cup again, he sported what Raine would describe as a blood moustache over his upper lip. Like a kid drinking milk for breakfast. The sight was fucking surreal.

"Is it good? Or do you prefer it fresh from the source?" Raine tried not to think about Thorne's teeth at his throat and the answering stiffness in his pants. He admittedly didn't know much about the assassin's feeding habits. He made a mental note to give Xander or Bailey a call. While he wasn't too keen on ending up as a snack, being bitten was a vital part of a claiming between mates and therefore a highly sexual experience.

Thorne rubbed a hand over his upper lip, then grinned and showed his fangs. "Are you volunteering, Red?" He made a weird purring sound. "What blood type are you? I prefer O negative."

Raine raised an eyebrow. "Did it take you long to acclimate to your new dietary needs after the treatment?"

"Treatment?" Thorne laughed harshly. "You've got my file on your lap, right? I bet you have someone in the Council delivering intel. Don't you know what happened after my therapy?"

Raine held up a single sheet and wriggled it. The other papers in the file were photos of Thorne's tattoos, taken while Thorne had been unconscious. "Bailey's knowledge about you is limited." The moment he'd said that and Thorne's grin widened, he wanted to snatch the words back. *Hell.* Thorne had no idea they had Bailey in their corner, did he?

"Fucking Atherton and his conscience. Was only a matter of time before the good doctor turned on us." Thorne didn't look worried. In fact, he showed no negative emotions about the betrayal.

"You must be pissed that he stabbed you in the back."

Thorne took another slow sip from his cup. He closed his eyes and rested his head against the wall. "Nope. I don't trust *any*one. Means I always expect random acts of backstabbing."

"Sounds lonely," Raine muttered. "You don't trust the men on your team?" He wondered who had fucked with his mate's head to cause such an attitude.

On the other hand, Raine had few people in his life he trusted wholeheartedly. Armand was one of those. But their friendship was also a double-edged sword because Armand's assignments were the main reason for Raine's issues.

Raine had hoped that, when he found his mate, he'd also find the one person deserving of his unconditional trust.

Thorne got up and stretched. "Me? Lonely? I can't imagine you have many friends either in your line of work. What do you tell them when they ask you about your day at work? *I'm fine, Laurel. I learned a fascinating new technique for effective waterboarding*," he said in a mocking voice. He fixed Raine with his dark eyes. "Because that's what you do, spy. Lie. Steal. Hurt people."

Raine swallowed. He usually felt bad thinking about the things he did for a living. But seeing Thorne's pleased expression, and hearing the pride in his voice, Raine felt a flutter in his belly. Cold dread closed around his heart like an iron fist. He didn't want to feel proud of his job just because it might be something Thorne—a killer—approved of. That would be sick, right?

Thorne growled low and deep. "Yeah. You can't tell me you never enjoyed extracting information. You've been part of the game for too long. I can see it in your eyes." Lowering to his hands and knees, he crawled toward the bars as he lowered his voice to a husky whisper. "But it's okay, because *you* followed orders. Like *me*."

Raine's head spun. Suddenly light-headed, he closed the file, his fingers shaking. Sweat trickled down his temple.

Thorne had done what Raine had tried to do to him—he'd uncovered his weak spot. This wasn't the first time a suspect tried to make the interrogation about Raine. If he weren't so overworked and bone tired, Thorne would never have gotten the better of him. Right?

Oh hell. Who was he trying to kid? Doubt had started to gnaw at Raine's conscience like a rabid animal long before he'd discovered Thorne.

Raine met Thorne's gaze through the thick bars and held it. "Very good."

"What?"

"Well, I expected you to be good at manipulating people. You're the leader of your team, after all. But how do you feel about being manipulated yourself? By Taylor? By Thoreau?" Raine slid from the chair and took a seat on the cement floor opposite Thorne. "They're using your abilities for their crimes against shifters."

Thorne shrugged and lowered his voice. "I signed a contract. It's not much different than working for the human government."

"You're killing innocent people." Raine tried to keep the indignation from his voice but failed.

Thorne lifted one eyebrow. "Exactly. Not much difference. Or are you naïve enough to think the government never orders innocents killed? I do as I'm told. I made a deal in order to cheat death. It would take a huge incentive to convince me to turn on the people who made that possible."

Raine took a deep breath. Finally he had an opening. "I know you had to be terminally ill for Taylor to include you in the program. What was it? Cancer?" According to Bailey, many assassins were suffering from terminal cancer when Taylor found them. Raine guessed it wasn't hard to troll a human hospital, throw out a net to cast for desperate people who'd do everything for even a couple more months, let alone a whole new lifetime.

Thorne's eyes narrowed.

"No cancer then." Raine racked his brain. "Navy Seal. I bet you had to crawl through bad places while serving in the military. Did you catch an infection during deployment? Bailey said you joined the program shortly after being discharged." Raine had to keep up the pretense of interrogating his mate, but all he wanted was to get to know the secretive man. Sharing facts about himself usually worked in getting people to open up, but he wasn't sure yet if he wanted to give Thorne so much power over him.

"Why is that important?" Thorne snapped. "What kind of interrogator are you? The coyotes asked about my missions and my team."

Oh, so he was getting defensive. Meant Raine had gotten too close to the truth. "An infection. Interesting. Something spectacular? Malaria? Ebola?"

Thorne lifted one side of his upper lip and snarled. His almost black eyes blazed with fury. This was the first spontaneous reaction Raine had seen on his usually stoic face. However, Thorne was right in saying Raine had been in the game for too long. And under Thorne's cold fury, Raine detected a deep pain that caused an ache in his own chest.

"We can talk about your missions, if you prefer a change of topic." Had this been any other prisoner, Raine wouldn't have backed down. He'd have used Thorne's slip to take him apart and bulldoze the walls he'd erected. "Give me something, and I'll make sure you receive another liquid snack."

Just that fast, the passive mask slid back over Thorne's face. "Good old bribery." He lowered his voice. "Boring, but fine. Let's make a deal. You deliver the snack yourself and I'll throw you a bone."

"Deliver it?" Raine frowned. "How?"

Thorne grinned. "You open the door and visit me in my

cell." His gaze flicked down to Raine's neck and back up again. "Don't look so shocked. You're not dumb enough to feed me from the source. Bring me a cup. Of your blood."

Raine scoffed. "Open your cell door? Not likely. I'm aware how strong you fuckers are." Thorne must not realize they were mates, wouldn't understand the importance of such a gift. If Raine entered his cell, Thorne might kill him and run.

"I've been Haas' guest for fifteen days. Means you have until tomorrow to change your mind." Thorne sounded bored, as though he didn't care what Raine decided one way or another.

"What happens after tomorrow?" Raine slid closer to the bars. He felt the electricity in the air, almost smelled it. "Wilder! Tell me."

A slow smile spread over Thorne's face. "My team is scheduled to assassinate an alpha who caused trouble for Thoreau in the past. Wouldn't you love to know the poor fucker's name?"

Shit. Although he knew for sure someone's life was in danger, Raine wouldn't take the risk of trusting Thorne. Hell, Donavan might skin him alive if he agreed to Thorne's offer.

"I can't. You know I can't."

"In the military, there are people responsible for delivering death notifications to relatives. Horrible job, don't you think? Did you ever have to deliver a death notification when a colleague died? Did you have to face a spouse while you told them their life will never be the same?" Thorne brought his face as close to the bars as possible. "Imagine how much worse it would be to face a mourning family, knowing you were responsible for their loved one's death, because *you* didn't have the balls to agree to my deal."

Oh, my mate is an even bigger bastard than me.

Raine thought of Jules, who'd almost died at his own brother's hand because Raine hadn't stopped Jonathan in time. There had been others, too. It wasn't possible to rescue everyone. Sometimes informants died. Sometimes informants got thrown under the bus for the greater good. And Raine wasn't dead enough inside to not care about those losses or forget about his involvement.

He lowered his voice to a whisper and noisily skidded his shoe over the concrete as he slowly got up, knowing the noise would conceal his words. "Here's the deal. I'll turn off the electricity and hand you the cup through the bars. Show me that I can trust you." Raine slapped his hands against his ass and the back of his thighs to dust off.

Thorne dipped his head once. "Looking forward to tomorrow."

Raine pivoted and strode down the hall. He'd maneuvered himself into deep shit. The wise thing would be to talk with Armand and tell him the truth. But then Armand might take him off the case and most likely keep him from seeing Thorne again. Someone else would take his place. Someone who didn't mind shocking Thorne into oblivion to get answers.

Over my dead body.

CHAPTER FOUR

Raine was sure he'd developed an ulcer. The mashed potatoes and half a steak he'd forced down lay heavy in his belly. Or maybe it was the lovey-doveyness around the dining table causing his queasiness.

London and Donavan were ridiculously cute together. London tried to fill his mate's already full plate with more food and Don kept looking at him with a mix of adoration and exasperation.

Gillian and Carol weren't much better with their mates, Gingham and Joseph.

Raine wanted to puke. He shot a look at Armand. His boss' cheeks were slightly red, and he was busy devouring Beta Cortez with his heated gaze.

Raine had seen Armand aroused before. Hell, Raine had once walked in on him fucking a cute blond over the back of a sofa—not something he ever wanted to witness again. But this was a business trip, and Cortez wasn't Armand's usual type. So seeing him salivate over the tall, dark, and brooding hunk was weird.

Raine wasn't blind to the subtle glances between Hugh and Raul, either. And didn't Orin, the veterinarian, and Francis look eager to drop their pants and forget their manners? The shy man had been introduced as Don's half-brother and the pack's accountant.

"Nothing yet?"

Raine looked up at Don's question and cleared his throat. "He's stubborn. I thought the prospect of more blood would loosen his tongue, but he knows how long he can go without while we have no clue. I asked Bailey. He said fourteen days is usually too long." He shook his head and pushed the rest of his steak across his plate.

"I watched you on the monitor this morning," Carol said. "Did he honestly offer to tell you who his team's next victim will be?"

Raine nodded and met Don's gaze. He'd briefed the alpha after leaving the prison.

"That's a deal we won't take. The stakes are too high." Don's voice booked no argument, just as Raine had expected. "The damn cell door only opens the day we carry his dead body through it. Or when he's sedated. Orin has knocked him out with his blowgun before."

Raine kept his face passive. Years of training and working as a spy kept him from slamming Don's forehead on the table for talking about his mate's death so casually. He needed help, but he didn't have anyone he trusted enough to ask for it. Armand, who usually knew everything about him, wasn't an option. His gaze fell on Hugh.

Hugh eyed him with sympathy.

Raine's breath caught. The deer shifter knew something. How, Raine had no idea. He knitted his brows in confusion.

Hugh slid his index finger along his coffee cup and tapped it several times. He dipped his head toward the kitchen and resumed eating.

Coffee? Kitchen? Ah, their chat on the porch. Raine dipped his head in acknowledgement.

"But what about the alpha who's in danger?" London asked. "It might be Xander. Hell, what if *you're* the target?" He wrapped one arm around Donavan.

Don sighed. "We'll increase the patrols. Xander's been informed. Many prides and packs have been affected by Thoreau's politics. It's impossible to figure out who exactly he targeted unless Thorne chooses to tell us." He focused on Raine. "I want you to increase the pressure. Armand told us about your methods. I was wondering why you've held yourself back so far. Use the damn stun gun." He peered at Orin. "We might have to sedate and shackle Wilder so Raine can get closer to the bastard."

Raine met Armand's gaze. His stomach turned when his boss nodded in agreement.

"Donavan's right." Armand cleaned his mouth with a napkin and leaned back. "Put the screws on." He regarded Raine coolly. "If it's too much for you, tell me honestly. You've been working non-stop for the past two years. I wouldn't think less of you for needing a break."

Now Armand offered him a break? He should've checked with him before he'd dragged Raine off to Pumpkin Creek. "I'm fine. It's only been two days. Earning a prisoner's trust takes time."

"We don't *have* time," Don snapped. "Not after Thorne's threat. To hell with his trust."

London hummed. "Maybe it's part of his game. Maybe he's eager to see what you're willing to do to make him spill his guts. Since we've confronted him with the horrible things he did in the line of duty, it's possible he wants to show us that we're not much better than him."

"Line of duty," Don muttered, his expression one of disgust. "He's not a soldier anymore."

Raine looked at London with new-found respect. Turned out he was more than a floppy-haired motor-mouth. "We have to take that into consideration, yes." Greater reason to detect whether Thorne was telling the truth before someone decided to torture him behind Raine's back.

"And he'd risk pain to play with us?" Don frowned heavily. "Why?"

Cortez snorted. "I talked with Bailey when he removed the

bullet from Thorne. If what he told me is true, Thorne's training was worse than anything we might do to him anyway. And still he feels loyal toward his bosses." He raised his index finger to his temple and circled it.

"Anyway," Don said. "Xander gave me a call. His tech guy Romeo and Beta Alan will come for a visit tomorrow or the day after. Alan will brief us on Finley and Vaughn's mission. He said they found a youth at the lab. Can you believe it? Aaron Shepherd. His older brother's an assassin as well." Don shook his head. "Romeo will check our electronic devices for spyware or something. Fin and Vaughn were attacked by a female assassin during a mission our enemies shouldn't have known about."

Carol gasped. "Is Vaughn okay?"

"More than." Don smiled faintly. "Finley Palmer's his mate. Vaughn's going to stay with the pride and take care of Aaron."

Raine grinned. "Wow. The sexual tension between them was so obvious even before they went on the mission. That's great news, right?" He looked around and wondered about the shocked expressions at the table. "What?"

Francis cleared his throat. "That is great news, Raine. We're all happy for Vaughn. His first mate, Walter, was our pack doctor. He was killed last year. For a while, we feared Vaughn would follow."

"Fuck. I didn't know." Raine rubbed his chest. He couldn't even begin to imagine what Vaughn had gone through. Cold dread pooled in his belly.

Thorne. What am I willing to sacrifice to save my mate's life? The answer was surprisingly simple. Everything. He met Hugh's gaze across the table. Raine's time was running out.

Although Thorne's cozy cell had no window, he always knew whether it was night or day. He felt it deep in his bones, a restlessness he couldn't explain, one that filled him with new energy. Well, the energy part was probably due to the blood he'd been given.

He rolled from his blankets to the naked concrete floor, preparing to work off the buzz in his veins with push-ups, when he felt a disturbance in the air. Something so subtle he almost missed it. *Some*thing was missing.

Thorne stood and sniffed the air. Aside from the effluvia of the deer shifters in the other cells, he didn't pick up anything. He sauntered toward the bars and listened. He was greeted by quiet. The constant hum he'd heard in the back of his head was gone. His eyes widened and he eyed the bars suspiciously.

This had to be a trick. Why would they suddenly turn off the electricity? Unless . . .

Thorne tensed when the door at the end of the hall snicked open. He fisted his hands in nervous anticipation when he recognized the gait of the person coming closer. His now familiar grassy scent hit Thorne a second later and made his mouth water.

Raine had ditched his suit and dressed in black jeans and a blue sweater instead.

Casual didn't suit him. Thorne preferred his personal interrogator buttoned up and proper.

Raine carried a paper cup. He was pale, and droplets of sweat dotted his forehead and upper lip. His scent held a subtle note. Fear? He should be afraid, since nothing but a row of useless bars separated him from a deadly predator.

"You brought my snack." Thorne dipped his head to the side. "In the middle of the night. Didn't think the coyote would agree to my bargain."

Raine's hand tightened on the paper cup. "Surprise."

Well, fuck me. Thorne was willing to bet his favorite knife that nobody was aware of Raine's stunt.

"The name of the alpha." Raine held up the cup. After a moment of hesitation, he came closer and placed one hand on the bars.

Thorne fought hard not to grin in triumph. He was as good as free. Reaching through the bars, he opened his hand. "After my snack."

Raine's throat muscles worked as he swallowed. He moved the cup toward Thorne's hand.

Thorne reacted with lightning speed. He grabbed Raine by the hoodie and yanked him forward so his head slammed against the bars.

Raine yelped and crumbled as he reached up to his nose. The cup hit the floor and splattered blood everywhere. "Ow! The fuck?"

Thorne retrieved the makeshift tool he'd made when he'd still had a real bed and slid it in the lock. It didn't take much to open the door.

The scent of blood from the spilled cup was too heavy in the air to ignore. However, Thorne had something better than the stale stuff available. He wouldn't pass up the opportunity, since he needed nourishment for his escape. And in case he was wrong and someone was still manning the video surveillance, he'd make the most of this before the guards were on him.

Thorne reached down and dragged a struggling, wriggling Raine over the floor to his blankets. "Come here. Time to get better acquainted, Red." He straddled him, grabbed a fistful of his black hair, and forced his head back.

"No! Please, don't kill me!" Raine's pale blue eyes were wide. He slammed his hands hard against Thorne's chest.

"Able-bodied food. I like it." Thorne grinned. Raine was broad in the chest, but no match for Thorne's altered genetics. Leaning over his prey, Thorne licked a line up Raine's neck. "Go on and fight me." He didn't have much time to play around. Still, he planned to enjoy his first good meal in ages. Raine's smooth skin tasted salty and musky. Thorne sucked at his neck for a moment and groaned. *Delicious.*

Raine bucked underneath him, proving he was a special kind of kinky.

Thorne ground his flaccid prick against Raine's hard-on and groaned. Time to get this over with. He bit Raine's neck, his eyes rolling back when the taste hit his tongue. To hell with O negative. This was pure ambrosia. Thorne sucked greedily, wrapping one arm around Raine in case someone was foolish enough to try and take him away.

Mine.

Raine made a weird choking noise. His hands found Thorne's back and fisted his wife beater. He moved against Thorne's body sensually as he babbled unintelligibly.

Thorne failed to make sense of his words.

"Thorne . . . please . . . don't . . . too much. Mate . . ." Raine slurred like a drunk.

Yeah, Thorne was taking too much. But Raine tasted so damn good, felt so good. His prick was so hard against . . . Shocked as though he'd been struck by lightning, Thorne slid his teeth from Raine's neck and took in the sight of his helpless prey. *That word.*

"What did you say?"

"Mate . . . feel woozy," Raine muttered. His bright eyes were tiny slits.

Mate. The word sliced through Thorne like a hot knife through butter. Taylor had made sure his assassins knew about a shifter's fate-picked mate. They not only cherished them above all else, they did dumb fucking shit to keep them happy. He'd witnessed it first-hand between Thoreau and Taylor. And on his missions. More than one mate had taken a bullet to protect Thorne's target.

Trust. Devotion. Forgiveness. Unconditional love.

Raine's hands slid from his back and flopped to the floor.

His eyes closed, and his breathing was shallow.

Thorne quickly bent over him and closed the oozing wound on Raine's neck with a slow lick. He sat up and cradled Raine against his chest in an unusually tender move. Thorne stared at his Red in wonder. "Shit. Fuck. Why? *How*?"

He was Raine's mate? A mate Raine was supposed to torture and hurt. But he hadn't. Instead, the dumbass had come to him to seal the deal, trusting Thorne would stand by his word. Trusting in the mate bond or whatever it was. "Foolish shifter," he muttered as he slid his fingers through the soft strands at Raine's temple.

Thorne eyed the open cell door, feeling unusually conflicted. He wouldn't get another chance. His grip on Raine tightened. He'd take it, but he wouldn't leave without . . . a hostage. Right. Red was nothing but a hostage. He tried to suppress the voice in his head screaming *mine*. Still, the intensity of their connection suddenly made sense.

Thorne hoisted Raine over his shoulder and left his cell. He brazenly walked past the wide-eyed deer shifters sitting in their cages.

"Hey!" Tobin, who occupied the last cell before the stairs, stepped close to the bars and curled his hands around them. "Be a decent guy and open the fucking cell doors."

Thorne stopped and showed his fangs. "I'm far from decent."

Tobin stumbled back a couple of steps.

Thorne eyed Tobin's rumpled appearance, the pleading and fear in his eyes. The deer shifter smelled of sweat and weakness. "It's no wonder Hector's operation tanked."

The locked door at the end of the hall wasn't any trouble. Keeping Raine over his shoulder, Thorne yanked the numeric keypad from the wall. He made quick work of separating the wires and twisting two of them together. He heard a snick, then the door clicked open.

"You fucking asshole! I hope the coyotes shoot you. Again." Tobin called after him.

Thorne ignored him as he quietly closed the door. He didn't know what awaited him upstairs. Given the fact he carried a guy over his shoulder whom he'd snacked from, he guessed whoever manned the monitors was asleep or dead.

Thorne climbed the steps and slowly opened the door. He peeked around it and found another hall. When no bullets came flying, Thorne snuck past closed doors.

He paused beside one door, smirking when he heard the unmistakable sound of two guys getting it on. Thorne wondered if the tryst was a coincidence or if Raine had somehow organized a distraction for the guards.

Thorne marched into a room containing a bank of monitors, a table, and a kitchenette. Shift schedules and printed memes were pinned to a corkboard. A couple of jackets hung from a hook rail beside a door Thorne hoped led outside.

Thorne grabbed one of the jackets and threw it on the table. Then he placed Raine on top of the jacket like a sleeping baby and dressed him. He quickly slipped into the other jacket before he picked up his prize again and left the prison.

The pitch-black night that greeted him was his friend, but he wouldn't underestimate the coyotes and their good noses and ears. Scouting the pack before the attack had taught him the farm and the houses were heavily patrolled. Not that he would mind meeting a patrolling coyote. Thorne needed a weapon. And shoes.

His lack of footwear became an advantage as he stole from one shadow to the next. He managed to avoid a couple of guards until he reached the edge of the farm.

Resting behind what he guessed was a shed for farming vehicles, Thorne placed Raine carefully on the ground. He pressed his back to the wall and listened for steps.

It took roughly five minutes before Thorne heard someone

coming their way. As soon as the woman came in sight, Thorne struck. He squeezed a spot between her neck and shoulder and caught her with one arm around her waist. Thorne laid her down. She had a handgun strapped to her hip. He grinned triumphantly when he found the knife in a holster around her thigh. He collected the weapons, then felt her pulse.

Steady.

One of her pack mates would find her soon, since they usually patrolled in teams of two. Thorne picked up Raine and, with a last look toward the farm, vanished into the night.

CHAPTER FIVE

Raine had the hangover of the century. He struggled to remember the last time he'd had that much alcohol. Maybe when he and Armand had tied one on after Armand had found a boyfriend photographing documents in his office in the middle of the night.

His damn head hurt as though a marching band was parading through his cranium—*and* they'd brought along the cymbals. His neck ached as well, so he'd probably slept in an awkward position. Groaning, Raine tried to touch his head but realized his hand was stuck. *Huh.* Both hands were stuck behind his back.

Raine peeled his lids open, bracing for more pain as soon as the light hit him. The room was dim, though. He lay on his belly on something softer than a blanket, but not as comfy as a bed. He slid his fingers over his wrist and encountered abrasive rope.

Damn. I'm not hung over at all. He'd been bound and dumped at an unknown place. In the dark. *Peachy.* Well, someone had closed the blinds on the windows, so it wasn't pitch black.

Racking his brain, he tried to remember where he'd last been. Dinner with the pack. Don mentioning Thorne's torture. He remembered his panic at the thought of Thorne dying. He'd made a deal with Hugh involving Roy the guard and a certain cocky cowboy who had the hots for Roy.

Fuck.

Groaning, Raine squeezed his eyes closed. The pain in his

neck had nothing to do with bad sleeping arrangements. Thorne Wilder, his own damn mate, had tried to drain him.

I've really won the love lottery.

"You're awake."

Raine rolled onto his back, wincing when the move put a strain on his shoulders and bound wrists. His eyes finally adjusted to the dimness, and he found Thorne sitting in a ratty armchair not far from him.

Thorne had managed to find jeans and the ugliest Christmas sweater ever, adorned with dancing reindeer and tight around his chest. He'd also found a razor, since his cheeks were smooth.

Raine shuddered at the thought of Thorne in possession of a razor and what he might do with it aside from cleaning up nicely.

Thorne was acting calm and controlled, not at all like a man on the run who was dragging an unwilling hostage with him.

Not that he's dragging me. Hell, Raine wasn't even an unwilling hostage. "Why?" He coughed and cleared his throat, then tried again. "Why?"

Thorne rose and then knelt beside him. "Because you gave me an opportunity I had to seize. Did you arrange the distraction for the guard?" Thorne reached for him.

Raine shrank back.

Thorne clicked his tongue and followed. He placed his hand under Raine's nape and lifted his head toward a . . . glass.

"Is that water?"

"Nah. It's battery acid." Thorne raised an eyebrow. "You know, because I couldn't have killed you a hundred times already." He placed the glass against Raine's lips and tilted it.

With no other choice than drinking or drowning, Raine opened his mouth and hummed happily when the water hit his parched throat. "More, please. I'm a little dehydrated." He shot his captor an accusing glare. "And where is *here* exactly?"

"Someone's weekend getaway, I reckon." Thorne stood and filled the glass from the sink in the tiny kitchen nestled in the corner of the room. "Or a summerhouse," he added as he looked around. Thorne returned and set the glass on the floor. He hoisted Raine into a sitting position and let him drink.

Raine licked his lips and panted, having guzzled the whole glass of water in one go. "More, please. Why did you take me with you?" No use denying he'd made it easier for Thorne to hightail it out of Pumpkin Creek.

Thorne filled the glass once more. He got down on one knee and regarded him silently for a couple of minutes while he gave Raine more sips of water. "How's your neck? The bite scrabbed over pretty quickly."

He met Thorne's dark eyes. They were so damn close, with him sitting on his ass and Thorne kneeling before him. His scent was all around Raine, making it hard to concentrate. Raine had heard tales about the mate pull. Experiencing it first-hand was wild. "Sore. We need to address your drinking problem, honey."

Thorne grinned, showing his fangs. "Assassins Anonymous? I'll make a suggestion to my boss. Honestly, how are you? Woozy?"

Raine frowned. While his dumb harpy chittered happily at Thorne's concern, Raine didn't trust it. "You want to know if I'm able to walk. So . . . no, I feel faint. Might take me a couple of days at an expensive spa to recover."

"No time to play fainting damsel. We're on the run from coyotes and cats. By the way, what are you? Please tell me it's something cute and fluffy. A bunny, perhaps?" Thorne smirked and bopped his nose.

"None of your business." Raine wriggled his nose and tugged at his bindings impatiently. "*You're* on the run, not me." He startled when Thorne suddenly cupped his face. "What are you doing?"

Thorne tipped his head back, leaning over him. The move pressed Raine's chest against Thorne's hard belly. "*We* are on the run. You and me, we're in this together. Don't think you'll ever get rid of me." He slid one hand slowly down the middle of Raine's chest. "I had your blood. You're mine. I'll find you, no matter where you go." Thorne slid his fingertips under the waistband of Raine's jeans—not touching him intimately, just teasing.

Raine sucked in a sharp breath and shuddered. He was caught in Thorne's gaze like a moth flying toward a flame. Being on the run with Thorne would burn his wings for sure. Was he a hostage, a plaything, or a living snack? Had Thorne figured out Raine had a soft spot for him? Thorne might want to torture him for information, but surely he wanted to reunite with his team and complete his mission as soon as possible.

Well, there was a thought. "The mission. Who's the target? You promised." Raine leaned up into Thorne's personal space. As much as he longed to feel Thorne's hand on his dick, he had to keep a clear head.

Thorne's nostril's flared. "Don't worry your pretty head. I'll take care of it. I'm a bastard, but I always keep my word."

Raine laughed. "Give me your word that you won't kill me."

"Deal."

"What?" Raine tensed when Thorne bent down and brushed the shell of his ear with his lips. Fuck, his damn scent was so strong. Raine took a long sniff of him and moaned.

Thorne growled quietly, wriggling his fingers under Raine's waistband. "You have my word that I won't kill you. Neither will any of my team members."

"I don't understand. What am I to you?" *Your mate, but I can't tell you yet.* "I'm not privy to Xander and Don's plans. I'm the guy who extracts information." Raine flinched when

Thorne stood and hauled him upright by the waistband. "You're giving my balls a wedgie. What now?" He swayed and, as he sank against Thorne's stone-hard chest, blinked quickly to chase away the stars dancing behind his eyes. "Whoa. Sorry. Need more fluids. You shouldn't have taken so much."

Thorne cupped the back of his head and looped his other arm around Raine's waist. The hold was weirdly tender, akin to the embrace of a lover.

Well, it would've been tender if it wasn't for the knife Raine felt pressed against his lower back. But with Thorne being an assassin, knives could very well belong in his erotic spectrum. Fuck, but the thought made him hornier than he already was. "Let go." Raine tried to twist free.

Thorne didn't give him an inch. "Stop wriggling," he whispered. He slid the knife between Raine's bound hands, and with a twist the ropes fell away. Stepping back, Thorne slipped the knife into a sheath attached around his thigh. He grabbed Raine's wrists and massaged the red chafing marks around them. "So I'm supposed to believe you when you say you can't tell me anything?" Thorne held his gaze, challenging him.

The soft circling of his fingers on Raine's bruised skin sent tingles down his spine, and he once again swayed toward his kidnapper. "Um . . ." *This is a really bad time to leak into my jeans.*

Thorne smirked. "You won't run from me."

A statement, not a question. Raine squinted. He swallowed around the lump in his throat. "What gives you that idea?" He pulled his hands from Thorne's grasp.

"Oh, please. You failed to torture me although you should've done that right away." Thorne recaptured his wrists and pressed harder on the red mark.

Raine hissed.

Thorne's eyebrows shot up. "Interesting."

Raine licked his lips. He tried to ignore his pulsing prick, but had to admit he was turned on by Thorne being all dangerous and murder-y. "So you understand my reluctance to torture and maim you as a declaration of undying love?"

Thorne slid his arms around Raine and cupped his ass. With a quick yank he pressed their groins together.

Raine became painfully aware that between the two of them, he might not be the only one with an obvious kink for danger. Clearly they'd need lots of lube . . . *if* Raine ever found the balls to tell Thorne they were mates.

"It's called lust, Red." Thorne's lips curled into a cocky grin. "I can smell it on you. I noticed that delicious scent the first time you came to me. Why do you think I jerked off for you? You *did* watch me, right?"

Raine growled, mad that Thorne had looked right through him from the start. "You bastard!" He punched Thorne's shoulder, cursed, and shook his hand. "What are you made of anyway? Concrete?" He tipped his chin up. "And don't look so haughty." He briefly closed his eyes when Thorne squeezed his butt. Raine lowered his voice. "You rubbed all over me when you had your fangs in my neck."

He winked. "My fangs are obviously not the only thing you want inside of you. But I don't have time to indulge. We need to go."

Raine shuddered. "Are you talking about your knife? And go where?" His brain was in shambles. His instinct to stick with his mate warred with his duty to return to Pumpkin Creek and Armand. He wriggled his hand between their bodies and cupped Thorne through his pants.

Thorne hissed. He pushed against Raine's hold for a second. Then he stepped around Raine and grabbed a backpack from beside the armchair. "I need to contact my team before they complete the assignment. I have a safe place where we can lay low for a few days."

"Lay low?" Raine scratched his head. He shouldn't be disappointed that Thorne had put distance between them—before he made a fool of himself and sank to his knees like a total slut. "I thought you'd rather meet with your team in person. Wait . . . you plan to hide?"

Thorne ran his gaze up and down Raine's body before he focused on his face. "Meeting my team's too risky."

Risky for whom? Raine? He was one of Thoreau's enemies, so it was reasonable that Thorne's team wanted to eliminate him. Thorne didn't seem willing to risk Raine's death. Raine wasn't sure whether he believed Thorne's vow to protect him.

He was startled out of his thoughts when Thorne closed a hand around his nape and pulled him close.

"At least try to focus on something else but your dick for a second, Red." His lips quirked up. "We're leaving. *Now.*"

For a spy and a shifter, Raine was as loud as a stampeding herd as he followed Thorne through a wooded area along a winding road. Thorne assumed Raine would've shown more grace without the blood donation. Since Thorne didn't sense anyone following close behind them, he refrained from grabbing his hostage and throwing him over his shoulder to silence those clumsy feet.

And he didn't need the temptation of Raine's pert ass so close to his face. He'd be too tempted to swat it or bite one of the perfect globes. Since the physical evidence for Raine's attraction toward him was piling up, keeping him at arm's length would become increasingly harder—no pun intended.

"Where exactly *is* your safe house? Please tell me you don't plan to walk there. I guess you have more than one, since your missions take you all over the country."

"Still in interrogation mode, Red?" Thorne kept his gaze and his ears on the road beside them. They needed a car and a cell phone.

Raine huffed. "I can't switch it off. Tell me. Since you insist on dragging me along, we're a team, and you owe me—" He yelped as he ran right into Thorne's back.

Thorne turned, grabbed Raine's arm and twisted it behind the man's back as he pulled him close. "A team?" He was taller than Raine by two inches, so meeting his startlingly bright blue eyes was easy. "Us being a team means you have to trust me completely. Can you do that?"

"Probably as far as I can throw you." Raine frowned. "Do your team members trust you completely?"

Thorne laughed at Raine's snarky tone. "They shouldn't." He wanted to take the words back, but they hung between them heavily.

"Right. The back-stabbing thing." Raine licked his lips. "But *I* should trust you? Give me one good reason." He tilted his head in a much too tempting maneuver.

Taking a deep breath, Thorne tightened his hold on Raine and lowered his voice. "Because by simply letting you live, I'm betraying my team's trust. My oath. That should *fucking* mean something to you." Shit. He hadn't meant to snap. Snapping meant he was . . . emotional.

Raine's gaze flicked over his face and finally settled on his lips. "Weirdly enough, I know exactly where you're coming from. I need to tell you . . ." He trailed off and frowned. "A car." He fisted the material of Thorne's sweater.

Thorne lifted his head. It took another couple of seconds before he detected the sound of an engine. "Damn. Are you a cat?" He'd learned that cat shifters had outstanding hearing. He grabbed Raine's hand and pulled him toward the road.

"No. And what the hell is your plan? You can't step into the middle of the road and stop a car."

Thorne shot his companion a look over his shoulder and grinned. Then he let go of Raine's hand and did exactly that.

He stopped in the middle of the road, placed his hands on his hips, and waited.

"Thorne!" Raine paced beside the road. "This is insane. Anyone stopping their car for a lone figure in the woods is probably a serial killer. If they're not, they'll be afraid you're one and they'll run you over."

"Calm down and save your breath for giving me road head. It's highly unlikely for two killers to meet each other on a deserted country road." Thorne concentrated on the car coming around the bend, a dark SUV. As soon as the headlights hit his body, the driver hit the brakes hard. The car swerved, slowing the closer it came to Thorne. With his superfast reflexes, Thorne wasn't afraid to get hit.

As soon as the car came to a stop a foot from Thorne, the driver's door opened and a man jumped from the car. "Are you fucking insane? What are you doing standing in the middle of the road, you . . ." The man, dressed in a gray suit, faltered as soon as he had a clear view of Thorne.

Thorne smirked and sauntered toward the man. "Good evening. I need to borrow your car." He heard Raine's steps behind him but didn't take his eyes off the driver.

The man laughed harshly. "What? You're trying to steal my car? Fuck off, you nut job." He flipped Thorne the bird and turned on his heel. He hurried back to the driver's door, but he stood no chance.

Thorne was on him in seconds. He grabbed the man in a headlock and squeezed lightly. The man wriggled. Thorne increased the pressure, cutting off the man's shout when he struggled to breathe.

"Don't kill him." Raine stepped around them. He met Thorne's gaze over the struggling man's head. "Don't. Kill. Him."

Being a professional killer, Thorne wasn't pissed that Raine thought the worst of him. Had he been alone, he'd probably have used the driver as a snack. But he didn't want Raine running away screaming, didn't want him to look at Thorne as though he was a monster.

Thorne squeezed until the human crumbled to an unconscious heap beside the car. He patted him down and found a wallet and a posh cell phone. Thorne pocketed the wallet and unlocked the phone by pressing the guy's thumb against the home button. "Get your ass into the car, Red." He quickly disabled the fingerprint lock mechanism.

"What are you doing?" Raine crouched beside the driver and felt his pulse. His shoulders sagged in what Thorne guessed was relief. "We can't leave him in a ditch. It's too cold."

Rolling his eyes, Thorne grabbed the driver and dragged him to the side of the road. When Raine tried to reach for the man, Thorne pushed him away and pointed at his chest. "I said get in the fucking car. Don't test my patience!"

Raine glared daggers at him, but he followed his order and slammed the passenger side door closed with enough force to rock the whole car.

Thorne sighed as he slid into the driver's seat. He shifted the car into drive and sped off. He punched in the number, then lifted the phone to his ear.

"Driving and talking on the phone at the same time is dangerous," Raine bitched. "You'll get us both killed. Or arrested. I'd love to see you in shackles." He crossed his arms over his chest.

Thorne ignored him and waited for the line to connect. When it did, nobody answered. They never did. "This is T4802 for P1639 on an insecure line." Out of the corner of his eye, he saw Raine staring at him with wide eyes. The handler redirected Thorne's call quickly. He heard two rings before a deep voice answered him.

"Commander."

"The mission has been compromised. Abort." When he didn't get an answer right away, he snarled. "You have anything to say, Priest?"

"The mission was canceled a fortnight ago when you were captured. You know the deal."

Fuck. Of course. Calling off missions was standard protocol. The bosses assumed they would give in and reveal their secrets under pressure. Dumb fuckers. Before he replied, Priest went on.

"Return to base. You're scheduled for a security briefing."

Thorne bit his tongue and tightened his grip on the steering wheel. "Understood. I'll need a couple of days." He disconnected and threw the cell in Raine's lap. "Call nine-one-one for the guy we left beside the road. Guess I don't need to tell you to use a fake name. Take out the card before you throw the cell."

"What was that?" Raine turned in his seat. "A chat with your team? Sounded very . . . affectionate."

Thorne considered their choices. Returning to base wasn't one of them. Even without Priest's cue, he'd crossed that off his list of options the moment he'd awakened in his cell. He'd rather die than willingly go through another *security briefing*. For all his talk regarding his loyalty to Taylor and Thoreau, he wasn't too keen on being tortured. Again.

The mission had been stopped. That meant another team would be sent. He had to inform Raine's pals who the targeted alpha was. Protecting her was up to the rebels. And then there was Raine . . .

Thorne listened with one ear while Raine talked with the dispatcher.

Raine lowered the window and tossed the cell into the night. "Okay. I want answers."

Thorne wished he had any to give. Cursing under his breath, he kept watch for signposts. He and the team had been in the area for a while before they attacked Donavan Haas's pack, so it shouldn't be too hard to find a way out of bumfuck nowhere.

"Wilder."

"Fine. We need to go to the safe house as fast as possible, pack some shit, and leave."

"What did your teammate say to you? Your whole body tensed up and you looked . . . spooked."

Thorne growled. Had it been anybody else, Thorne would've decked them for insinuating that anything had the power to spook him. But Raine was his . . . mate. If fate was to be believed, he was the other half of the soul Thorne had sold when he'd joined Thoreau's squad. They'd have to share Raine's soul from now on—however much the man had left after working as an interrogator and torturer. Fuck, they were a match made in hell.

"I'm not spooked." Thorne sighed. "When one of us escapes capture, we have to go through a security briefing."

"Let me guess. It's not a nice chat involving cookies and coffee."

"Not unless you consider it *nice* when someone uses hot coffee to waterboard you." When he saw a sign for Harrison, Thorne took the turn and followed the road.

Raine made a sound in the back of his throat. "Nope. Fuck. And here I thought you were eager to return to base or something. Back into the fold. They'll torture you because you were caught?"

Thorne nodded. "To make sure I wasn't turned by the rebels."

"Rebels?"

"You and your lot. Xander Powell. Donavan Haas. Thoreau calls them rebels who want to overthrow the current political system." He shrugged. "Not that I care about shifter politics."

Raine growled. "What *do* you care about? Money? Is that it? You pull the trigger for whoever pays?"

"How's the air up there?"

"Up where?"

"Up on your moral high horse, Mr. Torturer. I pull the trigger for those who gave me a second life." Thorne didn't feel the need to apologize for his actions. Not even to his . . . whatever. Raine would accept him the way he was anyway, like Taylor accepted Thoreau. Right? "At least until now."

"What is that supposed to mean?" Raine touched his leg.

Thorne placed his hand on top of it without second-guessing his action. "I'm not going through another adjustment. I never planned to return to base after escaping Haas' cell. Since you're with me . . . If I don't turn up in two days, they'll send my team after me." He pursed his lips. Chances were high they were lurking in the area. Fuck.

"Send your team? To take you back to base?"

Thorne laughed. Cute, foolish man. "To take me *out*. None of us get a third chance."

Raine gasped. "They'll order your team to kill you? And they'll do it?"

"Probably." Thorne waved his hand in the air in a maybe gesture. "It's the management's way to assure our loyalty. If the team refuses to kill me, they'll be liquidated next."

Deep down, Thorne was honest enough to admit it hurt to think of his team killing him. Despite their natural trust issues, he'd come to care for his men's wellbeing and relied on them to a certain degree. Especially Priest, his second.

"Wow. That's harsh." Raine was quiet for a while. "We're not trying to overthrow anything. The people you killed . . . they were trying to stop Thoreau from disabling our Council. Reliable sources have informed us that Thoreau wants to rule alone. Story as old as time. Rumor has it he'll introduce a law to make him president for life. Although I wonder why anyone would want to carry such a burden until death. He uses bribery, blackmail, and murder to ensure the councilmen's votes are in his favor."

Thorne sighed. He'd met Thoreau a handful of times and found him an unlikeable asshole. However, he hadn't struck Thorne as particularly eager to lead. He left a lot of the dirty work to his underlings. "Like I said, I don't care for shifter politics." It was obvious his man felt rather passionately on the matter. *Fuck.* "I need to disappear before the team finds me. And you'll come with me."

"Stop the car."

Thorne frowned. "I don't—"

"Stop the fucking car right the fuck now."

Thorne hit the brake.

Raine grabbed the oh-shit-handle and braced one hand on the dashboard.

They came to a screeching halt at the side of the road. Thorne put the car in park and turned in his seat, meeting a red-faced Raine's gaze. "What?"

"You kidnapped me. Fine. We're on the run from a team of killers who are also kinda your friends. Also fine." Raine raised his voice. "But I will not, I repeat *not,* run off with you and skip out on my fellow *rebels.*"

Someone should've warned Thorne that mates were a damn stubborn lot. He slammed his hand on the steering wheel. "This is not open for discussion. I heard Argentina is great this time of the year. I have money and passports hidden—"

Raine snorted. "You can't force me to abandon them and our cause."

"Your cause might get you killed."

"As though you care!"

Thorne's control snapped. He grabbed Raine by the fabric of his jacket and pulled him halfway across the center console.

"I kidnapped you *because* I care. Thoreau will eventually kill the rebels or cause a war among shifters. I can only protect you while you're by my side. *If* we're lucky enough to escape Priest and the others. I'm giving us a fifty-fifty chance."

Raine lowered his voice. "I thought I was a hostage. Why do you want to protect me?"

"You know the reason," Thorne murmured. He brushed his nose over Raine's cheek. "You know." Had Raine forgotten what he'd revealed because he'd been too overwhelmed by the feeding? Was he in denial because fate had given him a crazy whacko for a mate? Not that he wouldn't understand it.

Raine's chest rose and fell rapidly. "Thorne . . ." He placed his hand on Thorne's shoulder—just holding him, not pushing him away.

Thorne trailed his lips over the shell of Raine's ear. "Come with me. I can force you if you don't come willingly." His stomach roiled at the thought of forcing Raine to do anything. Trussing him up had been hot. Causing him pain, though? Never.

"They're my friends. Please." Raine cupped the side of Thorne's face. Their gazes met and held. "I need to do what's right. Not what's convenient."

Being the recipient of Raine's resolute look, Thorne felt a pressure in his chest that was either a sign of a heart attack or affection. He was unfamiliar with both. "Fuck. And what do you suggest? Do you want me to drive back to Haas and deliver myself on a silver platter?" The overwhelming need to please Raine left Thorne befuddled. The connection between mates obviously worked both ways, even if one wasn't a shifter. He hadn't taken that into consideration. He let go of Raine and stepped on the gas.

Raine sighed. "Of course not. I . . . don't want you to put yourself in danger. Let's go to your safe house and take it one step at a time."

Chapter Six

Raine spun on his heels and took in the sparsely furnished cabin. As creepy cabins hidden in the woods went, this one was exactly as he'd pictured. Spider webs in the corners and dust on all the furniture. The rough hardwood floors carried the scars of years of neglect. Clearly the maid's day off. "At least it's dry," he muttered. "And your team is unaware of your romantic hideaway? That's hard to believe." Raine kept a wary eye out for a bloody axe. *I'm sure there's one hidden around here somewhere.*

Thorne brushed past him on his way through the tiny living room with an even tinier kitchenette. "I didn't tell them, but of course they know. We don't have more than a couple of days." He pushed a door open and threw his bag inside. "Bedroom's through that door."

"I'll sleep on the sofa."

"You'll sleep with me. Not negotiable. Want a shower?"

Raine pursed his lips. Sharing a bed. Yeah, that sounded about as great an idea as rolling in honey and waiting for the bears to arrive. The tension between them had increased the longer they'd been in the car together. Raine wondered who'd snap and attack first. "This charming place has running hot water? My yelp review just went up a star."

Thorne grinned. "Didn't say it was hot."

Raine's eyes widened.

"God, you're easy." Thorne laughed. "Yes, there's hot water. I have canned food, or did you think I'd let you starve?"

"You can't afford to let me starve, since I'm obviously a

part of your food pyramid." Raine raised a hand and carefully touched the Band-Aid at the side of his neck. The bite had hurt at first, but when Thorne had started sucking . . . the sensation had transferred right to his cock. He guessed that was the same effect that made mating bites so pleasurable. Raine's enjoyment was most likely tied to their connection, since London had described Bailey's bite as pure hell.

Thorne was suddenly very close.

Raine took a step back and bumped into a chair. Thorne steadied him with a firm hand on Raine's arm. "And what a delicious morsel you are." He licked his teeth. "I don't need to take from you more than once a week. Your blood is . . . strong." His gaze dropped to Raine's neck. A faint red gleam entered Thorne's dark eyes.

"But you *want* more than once a week, right?" Mates always felt the strong urge to consummate their mating, even after the claiming. Sex strengthened the bond and—in the case of heterosexual couples and some rare bird shifter breeds—ensured many offspring.

Raine guessed that with Thorne, drinking blood would always be a part of their sex life. The thought that Thorne would take his nourishment from Raine for the rest of their lives was unbelievably empowering. Raine would be able to provide for his mate like no other shifter he knew. His harpy preened and fluffed up his feathers in his mind.

Thorne's hand on Raine's arm tightened. "That's not necessary." He let go and stalked toward the kitchenette, opened the faucet, and let the water flow while he grabbed a glass. He filled it, leaned against the counter, and drank with an intensity bordering on desperation.

Frowning, Raine crossed his arms over his chest. "Are you sure? You went without for so long during your captivity. Don't you need to . . . fill up your tank or something?"

"I'm not fully human, but I'm not a car." Thorne studied

the content of his glass intently. "Drop it."

Like hell. "You enjoyed it. We both did. Be*yond* a mere necessity that keeps you alive and kicking. Why would you deny yourself a pleasure—"

Thorne brought the glass down on the counter with a bang. "Why are you so eager to offer me your vein again? You fought against me, begged me not to take too much. And I might have if it wasn't for . . ." He growled and gave Raine his back. Thorne started opening and closing cupboards.

"What are you doing? Looking for words to make that last sentence seem less terrifying?" When Thorne didn't answer, Raine stepped closer. "If it wasn't for what? You can't ignore me when we're discussing my almost demise."

Thorne held up a can but didn't turn around. "Tomato soup okay? I'm afraid I don't have what it takes to make grilled cheese to go with it."

Raine reached around Thorne and pulled the can from his grip. He placed it on the counter then slid around, in front of Thorne. "I never understood the American habit of eating a cooked cheese sandwich with soup anyway. After two years of living in this country, I still cringe at the thought of dinner rolls smothered by a pale sauce that looks nothing like real gravy. For breakfast! Who in the ninth circle of hell invented such a culinary crime?"

Thorne gasped and pressed a hand to his chest. "Says the guy who was probably brought up on frog legs and snails drowned in herb butter."

Raine rolled his eyes and placed his hands on Thorne's waist. "At least we don't confuse dinner food with breakfast. A croissant and jam are perfectly fine choices to start the day."

"Maybe for a pencil pusher from the council who sits on his ass all day." Thorne stabbed a thumb at his own chest. "This little assassin needs a hearty breakfast."

Raine lowered his voice to a deep drawl. "Eggs and bacon,

turning men into efficient killing machines since eighteen sixty-five." He watched, fascinated, as a slow grin developed on Thorne's face.

Thorne guffawed, leaned over and actually giggled, then threw back his head and laughed. It was a deep laugh from the belly, full of joy and so honest that the beauty of it took Raine's breath away. Thorne held onto the counter with one hand while he lost it. "You . . . damn, Red."

Raine felt his face heat and chuckled quietly. He bet nobody had seen Thorne laugh freely in several years. If ever. The man wasn't cheer personified. And while Raine wasn't either, there had been a time in his life when he'd loved to joke around and make his friends and colleagues laugh. Before duty, regret, and pain had slowly taken over his life and snuffed out that joy inside him.

Thorne brushed tears from his cheeks, still emitting muffled laughter.

"Why are you calling me that?"

"What?"

"Red." Raine shrugged. "I mean, my real surname is also used as a nickname for someone with red hair. But I'm not a redhead, so I'm confused."

Thorne regarded him silently for a moment. "Your shirt."

"Excuse me?"

"When you visited me the second time, you wore a blood red shirt. So very teasing. So tempting," Thorne murmured as he laid a hand over Raine's sweater-covered chest. "Wearing that shirt was equivalent to waving a flag in front of a bull."

Raine swallowed. "And then the bull attacked."

Thorne made a non-committal sound in the back of his throat. "What else does your name mean? Rousseau. I was crap at school, but wasn't he some smart dude in your country?"

"He was a philosopher and writer. Believed that the

natural goodness of humankind was warped by society."

Thorne's gaze met his. "That's horrifyingly fitting." He slowly tugged Raine against his chest. "Do you think your namesake is right? Was there natural goodness inside me until I let society ruin me?"

Once again Raine was surprised at Thorne's touchy-feely behavior. On the other hand, he shouldn't be. Thorne's bite had started the bonding process. They were both helpless against the pull.

Raine stretched his arms over Thorne's wide shoulders and linked his wrists behind his head. "I believe everyone is born with both goodness and malice. It's what happens to us after birth that tests our inclination to be good or bad or . . . a little of both." He shivered when Thorne's big hands splayed on his back.

Raine was sure Thorne felt the deep connection between them grow stronger with every minute. He doubted Thorne was an affectionate man with the habit of cuddling hostages. The readiness with which he accepted Raine's affection had to be a result of the mating bond.

"My combat-booted feet are firmly planted on the bad side of the fence, don't you agree?"

Raine cupped Thorne's nape with his hands and squeezed lightly. "I cut the electricity on that fence and opened the gate today. What happens next is up to you." What Raine wanted to say was *please help me and my friends defeat Thoreau and save shifterkind*. He didn't, since he had no more right to ask this of Thorne than his mate had in asking him to join the fight against the rebels. But the thought must've been visible on his face.

Thorne groaned and briefly closed his eyes. "That's your way of giving me a big fat *no* on my Argentinian escape plan." He pushed Raine away and pulled a pot from the cupboard.

Frustrated, Raine ran a hand through his hair. "Of course

it is. Innocent people are dying, Thorne!"

"You must have me confused with someone else."

"Who?"

"Someone who cares," Thorne snarled. When he turned, he held a can opener like a weapon. In Thorne's hand, it probably was.

Raine crossed his arms over his chest. "Wow. Hey, if I stake you through your heart of stone, will you die like the vamps in the movies?"

Thorne blinked, looking surprised for a second, before he grinned. "Everyone dies when you stab them through the heart with a wooden stake, Red. Nothing particularly vampiric about it." The humor slowly fled his face, replaced by resignation. "Let's quit the bullshit for a second. What do you want me to do? Be honest. If you could ask me anything . . ."

Raine held his mate's gaze. "I want you to help me end Richard Thoreau's reign of terror." God, he hoped this wouldn't blow up in his face.

"And how far are you willing to go for this sacred goal? As far as Thoreau himself? By asking me to do what I'm good at and kill him?" Thorne raised a brow. "Only, I'd proceed differently. If you ask me to render Thoreau useless, I'd do something worse, because I'm a bastard. Wouldn't be the first time I stooped that low either."

Raine swallowed around the lump in his throat. What could be worse than ending Thoreau's existence? "I don't understand."

"I would deliver Zane Taylor's lifeless body to Thoreau's doorstep and watch him break over his precious mate's death. That's the sort of man I am. So you better think twice before asking for my help in this matter." Thorne's eyes were flat black pools.

Icy cold flooded Raine's body as he struggled for a response. Knowing your mate was a killer and hearing what he was capable of doing were two completely different things. Thorne's clinical description of what he'd do to Thoreau shocked him to the core. And then one word in particular hit him like a brick to the head. "Mate? You know that Taylor is—"

"The president's mate? Sure. They're fucking behind Thoreau's wife's back. Don't know why he has a wife anyway if he's got a mate."

Raine's hands shook. "What . . . what do you know about mates?" If Thorne was familiar with the concept, it wouldn't take him long to understand the reason for Raine's softness toward him.

Thorne closed the distance between them and brought his lips to Raine's ear. "Everything, Red. Why do you think I was unable to leave you in the cell when I escaped? Ask me to kill for you, and I'll do it. But you'll have to live with the consequences. You'll have to live with the knowledge of what I'm capable of."

He knows. Oh my God, he knows about us.

Raine retreated, avoiding Thorne's gaze. "I think I'll take a shower. Excuse me." He was running, so sue him. His thoughts were a mixed-up, jumbled mess in the big useless organ that had been a perfectly functioning brain before he'd met Thorne Wilder.

Raine hurried into the bathroom, slammed the door behind him, and rested his back against it. He didn't bother turning the lock. That would be useless if Thorne wanted to come inside anyway.

He knows we're mates.

With that came another realization. Thorne's reluctance to join the rebels' fight against Thoreau might have nothing to do with his disinterest in shifter politics. Although Thorne believed himself to be a monster, he didn't want Raine to see him as such. He'd been trying to remain impartial—not doing Raine's bidding, but also refusing to leave him behind.

Instead, he'd asked Raine to run away with him. Thorne had asked for a new start. For them. Together. While Raine had tried to convince him to switch sides.

Raine raised his hands to his face and groaned. Fuck, but his murdering mate had more honor than he did.

CHAPTER SEVEN

Thorne had heated the soup, ladled it into two bowls, and waited for Raine to finish his shower. Raine had finally emerged, skin pink from the hot water, a towel wrapped around his hips. Thorne had almost swallowed his tongue when Raine sat down opposite him.

Raine looked like those guys in the deodorant advert, the ones who dropped from heaven. He only lacked the wings. Thorne bet feathers would suit this man. Black ones, because there was no angelic innocence in Raine's seductive swagger. Raine was temptation personified, like that fallen angel in the series Priest binge-watched on their days off.

Thorne had barely made it through their meager dinner without throwing Raine on the table and having his way with him. As soon as the bowls were empty, he'd excused himself to the bathroom.

Now he stood under the shower, hands braced against the wall, cold water pelting his back.

There wasn't much Thorne was afraid of. The prospect of his team hunting him was a mere inconvenience. The thought of Taylor's briefing a pain in the ass.

No. What filled him with dread was the possibility of losing control with Raine. Thorne was fucking strong. A predator who hunted, captured, and eliminated. He was hard and rough, his desire for Raine a gnawing hunger in the pit of his stomach that surpassed his need for blood tenfold. He'd grown used to the thirst, learned how to tame it.

Thorne wasn't afraid he'd drain Raine. He didn't worry

Raine would leave him because he was a killer and a bastard of epic proportions. Thorne was terrified he'd hurt Raine during the sex Raine's gaze had promised over dinner.

After his diagnosis, his sex drive had dwindled. The stuff he'd seen and experienced during his training as an assassin had killed it for good. Or so he'd thought. Thorne had buried his unnatural desires under years of denial and convenient erectile weakness. The sudden sexual need he felt for Raine was . . . terrifyingly strong.

Eventually they would succumb to the tension crackling between them—that was inevitable. Thorne had jerked off to thoughts of Raine in his cell, had imagined fucking him in the car and during dinner. He'd be unable to . . . control himself.

The decent thing would be to talk with Raine. But what man wanted to admit he was fucked in the head when it came to sex? On the other hand, he'd confessed all kinds of other disturbing shit. What was one more nail in the coffin in the grand scheme of things?

Thorne shook his head and made quick work of washing himself. Chances were, despite the half-naked dinner episode, Raine wouldn't welcome Thorne's touch after he'd revealed being a mate murderer. Granted, Thorne had only done it once on purpose. The other times had been . . . accidents.

After he shut off the water, Thorne stepped from the shower and toweled himself dry. He dumped the scratchy towel on the floor, then opened the door and left the bathroom.

Raine wasn't in the living room. Thorne froze briefly. A faint rustling sound came from the bedroom. Relief flooded him, since he wasn't entirely sure what he'd do to Raine in case he decided to ditch Thorne. The options ranged from tying him to the bed to spanking the snot out of him.

It had been a long and taxing day, so Thorne was prepared to slide between the sheets and sleep for a couple of hours.

What he found on the bed wiped every thought of sleep away.

Raine lay sprawled on the thin comforter in all his naked, pale-skinned, muscled glory. His nipples were tiny brown peaks in the chilly air. And, damn, the skin of his groin was smooth.

A non-definable sound broke from Thorne's throat. "What the fuck? I tell you what I'm capable of and you offer yourself like a sacrifice? What's wrong with you?" And what was wrong with Thorne that he wanted to talk things out instead of taking what was so obviously his?

Raine rolled his eyes. "Go on and give me a complex. I'm merely chilling." He smiled, but the smile didn't reach his eyes. His skin was suspiciously sweaty in the cold air.

"Are you afraid of me?" Thorne walked to the bed and placed one knee on the mattress. "I didn't get an angsty vibe from you when I actually threatened you. So who's giving whom a complex? Although I have to admit, I'm a big messy ball of complexes when it comes to . . . this." He waved his hand back and forth between them before he finally climbed on the bed.

"This?" Raine arched a brow.

Not seeing a point in beating around the bush, Thorne moved over Raine in one smooth glide. He hissed when his skin touched Raine's. He had to admit, they looked stunning pressed together. Black and white. Two sides of a coin. Both of them being more or less bad guys, neither of them even remotely good, although Raine probably prided himself in being on the side of the good guys.

"You're not fighting against me. Why?" Thorne met Raine's gaze and watched him slowly tilt his head, silently asking for a kiss. Raine, Thorne realized, was probably the only person who wouldn't stab him in the back, because of the mate thingy that connected them. Considering the guilt Thorne had laden on himself, Raine's trust was more than he deserved.

"You know why."

Raine was so close his breath fanned over Thorne's lips.

"And you had to know this would happen when you revealed your knowledge concerning mates. What are you bad at?" He slid his palms over Thorne's upper arms.

Thorne shuddered. While he enjoyed the soft touch immensely, his cock remained stubbornly uncooperative. No surprise. "Interpersonal relations. Really bad at them."

Raine snorted. "It's called sex. While I was undercover for two years, I paid a discreet escort service so nobody at the office would see me with a guy. I was deeply unsatisfied because I'm usually not into . . . casual sex." He trailed the tip of his index finger over the bone frog tattoo crawling up Thorne's arm.

Thorne growled and rolled onto his back. He was surprised when Raine followed him and pressed against the curve of his body. He slid his hand down Raine's back and cupped his butt carefully. The tight cheek was like marble under his fingers. Thorne remembered Raine's reaction to the chafe wounds around his wrist. Closing his eyes, the need to redden Raine's perfect flesh overwhelmed him. His urge caused a twitch in his nether regions.

Raine shuddered. "You're . . . not hard," he whispered.

"Don't have to be to make you scream." Thorne ran his index finger through Raine's cleft. Some playing wouldn't hurt, right? To bring Raine the pleasure he obviously sought. They didn't need full-on penetration to have fun anyway, and it would be easier for Thorne to control himself if he left his cock out of the game.

Raine hissed and wriggled. "Yes. Touch me."

"Thought I was your enemy. You want my finger in your ass?"

"Or two or three." Raine latched onto his neck and sucked.

"You make me weak. The moment I looked into your eyes I wanted to kneel before you and—"

Thorne snapped and shoved Raine onto his belly.

Raine grunted. "Oh fuck. Finally."

Thorne knelt beside his mate. He placed his hand on the small of Raine's back and ran it slowly up his spine. "Marvelous muscle definition. You're a work of art. Strong. Fierce. Cunning."

"Huh." Raine curled his fingers into the sheet and rolled his back toward Thorne's touch.

"Touch-starved?"

Raine snorted. "There's only so much I'm willing to let a prostitute do to me. With you, though . . ."

Thorne reached Raine's neck, hesitated, and then grabbed his hair. "No kneeling today." He yanked at the silky black strands and smiled.

Raine moaned. His eyes slid shut, and a lovely blush colored his pale cheeks.

"I've got you." Thorne bent over and pressed kisses to Raine's pale shoulder. "Tell me what you need me to do for you. It's yours."

"Fuck . . . Thorne." Raine's breathing sped up. His damp skin glistened under the light from the bedside lamp. "My . . . bird needs a claiming."

Thorne shook his head, vowing to ask Raine what breed of bird shifter he was later. "We haven't started yet, but you're all hot and bothered already." He rested his free hand on Raine's ass. "I've heard of claiming. Are you sure you want to tie yourself to a killer?"

"Mates . . . need to claim." Raine licked his lips, pulling Thorne's attention to his plush pink mouth that would look stunning around his prick. "You started the process when you snacked on me. One of us needs to come inside the other to seal the claim. My scent should make you hard. I don't understand—"

"Hush. Later," Thorne murmured, meaning the blowjob as well as the claiming. No chance in hell would he spill inside Raine tonight. And he wasn't close enough to dealing with his baggage to let Raine fuck him. He had to distract them both. "Trust me. We'll start easy." He forced Raine to turn his head and brushed his index and middle finger over Raine's lips. "Be good for me and get them wet. You didn't answer my question anyway."

Raine smirked before he poked out his tongue and lashed it over his fingers.

"That's not nearly enough for where those digits are gonna go." Thorne added a growl to his voice. "Try harder." He loved the shudder running through Raine's body.

"Fuck." Raine sucked Thorne's fingers into the wet heat of his mouth. He closed his eyes as he moaned around them. The longer he slurped, the more effort he put into the task.

Thorne's dick started filling. Raine's agile tongue would feel marvelous bathing his prick. "You're a natural. Very eager. But please refrain from telling me where you learned this. I don't have the time to chase down your past conquests and off them."

Thorne pulled his fingers from Raine's mouth and brought them back between his cheeks, seeking his entrance. When he found the tiny pucker, he pressed gently until Raine's moans and wriggles reached the perfect height of desperation. Only then did he slip his middle finger through the stubborn ring of muscles.

Raine's eyelids fluttered. "More! Damn you. I'm not going to break."

"You're so incredibly tight. How many times do you think I can bring you to the edge until you shoot over the sheets?" Thorne mused, watching Raine's face as he added a second finger.

"Oh fuck. Evil bastard." Raine panted.

"Answer my question and I'll give you a third." Thorne curved his fingers.

Raine's pretty eyes rolled, and he made a choking sound. "I hate you! How am I supposed to remember the stupid question?" He clenched around Thorne's digits, moving a hand slowly down to his dripping prick.

"Don't you dare touch my property." Thorne used the voice he usually reserved for training new assassins. During training, he'd never felt the sense of satisfaction that filled him when Raine spread his arms on the bed obediently and gripped the sheets. "Are you sure you want to tie yourself to a killer?" He spat on Raine's beautifully spread hole and added a third finger.

Raine groaned. "Yes! Will never desire anyone as much as you. We're in this together, so I might as well give in before we're killed by your team. For once in my life, I want . . ." He turned his face into the bedding, but the move didn't hide the blush spreading over his neck and face.

Thorne bent over and nibbled teasing kisses along Raine's shoulder blade. "What do you want?"

"I wanna be selfish," Raine mumbled. He shifted and looked over his shoulder. "Just once I want to forget duty and do what feels right for *me*. *You* are right for me. Let's face it. We'll probably die anyway over the next couple of days. I want to know what it feels like to be bound to the one person created for me."

The open vulnerability, the longing in Raine's gaze broke something inside Thorne. Cursing quietly, he slid his fingers from Raine's chute and rolled him to his back. Seeing the confusion flickering over Raine's face, Thorne quickly moved over him and between his legs. "Permission to jerk yourself. Do it. Show me." He pressed his mouth to Raine's, licking and biting at his lips until Raine opened up for him with a soft whimper.

Raine slid his hand between their bodies and started beating off frantically. He curled his free arm around Thorne's neck and held on tight. Then he brought his strong legs up and around Thorne's hips.

Thorne ran his hand over the bend of Raine's leg and up until he cupped his marvelous ass. All the while, he never took his gaze off Raine's hand on his angry pink prick. "Perfect, Red. You're stunning in your need." He brought his fingers back to Raine's entrance and unceremoniously pushed them back inside Raine's warm hole.

Raine's breath stuttered. His expression was a mixture of pain and pleasure that was probably due to Thorne's harsh fingering. He bit his lip so hard it bled.

The red smear on Raine's lips pushed Thorne off the cliff. His prick hardened while his gaze was fixed on the drop running over Raine's pale skin. Bending down, Thorne licked the trace of blood away and moaned. "You are the sweetest drug." Fighting against his urges, he pressed his face against the sweaty crook of Raine's neck and took a deep breath.

Raine's freshly mown grass scent catapulted him momentarily to his past. Back to happier days. Thorne shuddered. Forcing himself back to the present, he slid a fourth finger past Raine's rim.

Raine squeezed his eyes shut and, with a roar, shot over his chest. He clenched around Thorne's digits.

Thorne made sure to rub the special bundle of nerves until Raine squirmed and pushed against his chest. "We're not done yet." His dick demanded his attention, but Thorne refused to give in.

Raine looked at him as though he'd lost his mind. "Can't remember the last time I came that hard." He panted harshly and tightened his grip on Thorne's neck. "I'm afraid I'm done for at least . . . what are you doing?"

Thorne ran his index finger through the seed on Raine's chest. Holding his mate's gaze, he sucked the digit clean and hummed. "You mentioned coming inside me."

Acting on instinct, Thorne scooped up more of the white cream and brought his hand back and around himself. He slid his finger over his hole before he pushed the tip inside. Thorne chuckled when he saw Raine's scandalized expression. "What?"

"Fuck, that's so hot," Raine whispered.

"Yeah. But will it work?" Thorne wriggled his finger deeper, slowly getting used again to the feeling of fullness.

"Only one way to find out." Raine coated his fingers in more cum and brought them to Thorne's cleft.

Not sure if he'd be able to take more than one or two fingers without freaking, Thorne pulled out and trusted Raine to go gently. He wasn't disappointed. Thorne rested his forehead on Raine's chest, delighting in the slow motions Raine used to push his seed into Thorne's chute.

Raine had long, slender fingers that felt absolutely perfect. And the kisses he pecked on Thorne's temple didn't hurt either.

Thorne moaned softly. Although it would take more time for him to truly feel comfortable with ass play again, he enjoyed giving Raine such intimate control over his body. Even his dick flexed. He rubbed against Raine's smooth balls. He grinned triumphantly when Raine nudged his prostate and his dick gave another enthusiastic jump. "Yes." Thorne was no fool. He knew his body too well. It wasn't the finger up his ass or Raine's magical shifter seed causing his shaft to fill.

The scent of Raine's blood hung heavy in the air. But maybe—just maybe—his stiffy was at least due to the trust he felt radiating from Raine. A trust Thorne returned. And maybe it was the gentleness of Raine's embrace.

"I need to bite you," Raine whispered against his head.

Thorne caught Raine's lips in a quick, sloppy kiss—tasting ambrosia once again—then leaned up and craned his neck. He'd never offered his throat to anyone. Especially not since he'd become an assassin. "Do it. Claim me."

Raine didn't hesitate. His teeth broke skin.

The pain sent an unexpected rush through Thorne that settled in his balls and made him ache for release. "Aww, fucking hell." When Raine sucked at the wound, Thorne sought the friction Raine's abs provided for his leaking prick with desperate intensity. Apparently, as long as blood was involved, it didn't matter which of them was bleeding for Thorne to get off.

Raine angled his fingers to brush Thorne's prostate again and growled. When he let go of Thorne's neck, a warm tickle ran down his skin.

Thorne's hips stuttered as he rubbed the head of his cock over Raine's skin once again. His breath caught in his chest. Then his balls pulled close to his body and forced an eruption of seed to mix with the mess on Raine's belly. "Holy . . ." Thorne gasped. His muscles spasmed while he rode the high of his climax. All the while, he was vaguely aware of Raine's hands on his back and shoulders.

When Thorne's arms gave up and he slumped on top of his mate, Raine let out a *hmpf* but chuckled.

"Heavy fucker."

The insult sounded weirdly affectionate. Thorne peeled one eye open, meeting Raine's amused gaze. "You broke me."

"That's a compliment I can return wholeheartedly," Raine whispered.

Thorne sighed deeply and relaxed in Raine's hold. The past two days had changed his life irrevocably. He was at a crossroads and had to face the facts. A selfish bastard by design, he'd never give up what he'd found in Raine. Thorne could either follow the plan he'd made and most likely alienate his mate by forcing him to leave the country. Or . . . he could make a new plan. Thorne was good at planning. He just had to make sure they both stayed alive.

CHAPTER EIGHT

Raine zipped up his jacket and jammed his hands into the pockets. Trudging through the woods after his mate, his efforts to preserve warmth were fruitless. Moisture hung heavy in the air and slithered between the layers protecting his body.

The fog that had greeted them when they'd left the cabin in the morning clung to their clothes, dense and suffocating. Water dripped from leaves and needles and coated the ferns they brushed aside in their passage. And although it was the middle of the day, it was fucking gloomy, thanks to the thick trees and the gray mist hanging in the air.

While the weather pissed Raine off, his harpy was happy as fuck thanks to the claiming and the constant presence of their mate. Raine fixed his gaze on Thorne's broad back and hard ass and suppressed a teenage sigh. He was afraid that—despite their difficulties—he was already utterly in love with his fangy murder-muffin.

"Explain to me again why we left the car behind?" Rationally, Raine knew the answer. Hell, had he been on a mission alone, he'd have done the same damn thing. But he was in the mood to bicker and complain.

Thorne was annoyingly patient today. He threw a look over his shoulder and smiled. "Don't make me explain the obvious, Red. We'll find another car soon enough. Aren't you enjoying our hiking trip?"

"If this *was* a hiking trip, I'd be fine. As it is, I'm wet and miserable. Countless people are looking for us to either kill us or lock us up. Hell, I feel like Richard Kimble convinced me to jump down the dam wall with him."

Thorne grunted. "That makes you Sam Gerard. The actor who played him was hot in that role. Brooding and . . . constantly annoyed. Fits you."

Raine picked up a stick and threw it at Thorne's back. He smirked when Thorne turned with an incredulous expression. "What? It wasn't a wooden stake."

"Don't make me place you over my knee," Thorne drawled.

"Right in the middle of nowhere? Bullshit." Still, Raine couldn't suppress the shiver of excitement at Thorne's threat. Last night, he'd noticed the exact moment Thorne's cock had joined the party. Having his own kinks, Raine wasn't one to shame another for their preferences. Especially not his mate. Considering Thorne's dietary needs, Raine knew they wouldn't have any trouble keeping things . . . *up*.

Thorne snorted. "Don't tempt me. I'd rather not stumble across my team while we have our pants around our ankles."

Raine lifted his shoulders to his ears and checked the path behind them. "You think they're close?"

"I trained them." Thorne stopped a moment until Raine was beside him.

"That's a yes." Raine sighed. He was surprised when Thorne's fingers brushed against his.

Thorne took his hand and squeezed. "We'll find a phone, call your boss, and give him the name of the targeted alpha."

"And then we wait for Xander's hacker to locate us?" Romeo Gatti wouldn't need more than five minutes to find them and send a team to pick them up. Question was, would Thorne agree to return with the rebels? "I don't expect you to work for us. You have my word."

Thorne jerked him to a stop and faced him. He lifted his hands and cupped Raine's face. "Why?"

Raine blinked. "You never once forced *me* to work for the other side. What kind of mate would I be if I . . ." He licked his lips. "You probably have valuable inside information that could help us in our battle against Thoreau. But you . . . we . . . what we have . . . is more important. As a spy, I went against my own beliefs so many times and barely recognized myself in the mirror. I'm so done with that shit. You were willing to leave the fucking country to protect me. I don't want to wake up one morning and find you gone because I put my job above your needs."

Thorne suddenly pressed his lips against Raine's. He groaned like a wounded animal while he plundered Raine's mouth.

Raine held on tight, clutching Thorne's jacket and giving as good as he got. He grabbed Thorne's ass through his jeans and yanked him close. A jolt rocked through Thorne. A muffled, pained-sounding noise left his lips. Raine grinned into their kiss, eager to take things further, when suddenly Thorne fell against him.

Trying to keep them upright, Raine lost his footing on the slippery, mossy ground. He turned them while they fell so Thorne's bulk wouldn't crush him, and landed beside his mate. "Wilder?"

Thorne's eyes were squeezed closed, his face a mask of pain. "Run," he pressed through thin lips.

"What are you—" Raine yelped when Thorne pushed against his chest.

"I said run! Don't look back." Thorne rolled onto his back and drew a gun. He lifted it, his gaze scanning the area. "Now."

That was when Raine saw the red blooming on Thorne's leg. "You're shot!"

"Thanks, Captain Obvious," Thorne gritted through his teeth. "I don't think we can consider this a hunting accident.

They're here."

Raine lifted Thorne's upper body, ignoring his protests, and sat behind him. He wrapped both arms around Thorne's chest and brought his lips to his ear. "If you think I'm leaving you behind . . ."

"Red. You're being unreasonable." Thorne's concentration never wavered from the trees before them. The fog made it impossible to see farther than a hundred feet.

"Shifter. We never leave our mate behind." Raine considered shifting. But whoever had shot Thorne might shoot Raine in the middle of his shift. And the close standing trees would be a disadvantage for his huge bird.

Thorne placed his free hand on Raine's leg and squeezed. "Let me talk." He sounded resigned.

Raine held him tighter. "Why haven't they killed us? Why the shot to the leg?"

Thorne chuckled, but it wasn't a happy sound. "Cross." He said it loud enough to carry through the fog. "A nice through-and-through. Thanks for not shattering my shinbone."

Tensing, Raine waited for the mysterious Cross to emerge from the fog. When nothing happened, he took a deep breath. "They're playing with us? Really?" That was both cruel and cunning. If that was how his mate trained his team . . . They were a match made in hell.

"Playing cat and mouse is *not* how we usually deal with our targets." Despite the cold, sweat popped out on Thorne's forehead. He grunted and wriggled, then hissed.

Raine rubbed his chest in soothing circles. Thorne must be in a hell of a lot of pain, but the hand holding the gun never wavered. Raine ran one hand down his mate's leg and carefully retrieved the knife from its sheath. He wasn't so dumb as to demand Thorne part with the gun.

"You won't need a knife, little bird," a melodic tenor said from the wall of fog. Slowly, a silhouette took shape until a tall blond man—clad entirely in black—appeared. He was lean and walked with the predatory gait of a cat. The hand holding a pistol hung relaxed beside his thigh. Thorne possibly shooting him didn't seem to worry him.

Why became obvious when two more figures cleared the fog and joined them. They were dressed similar to the first. A golden badge adorned their left arms. One man was a tall African-American, his skin darker than Thorne's. Raine couldn't count the knives strapped to his body. The other was shorter and of Middle-Eastern heritage. Although Raine didn't see any weapons on him, that didn't mean he didn't have them.

"Lance." Thorne's throat worked as he swallowed. When he turned his gaze toward the black man, he lowered the gun a smidge. "Priest."

Ah. Thorne's second-in-command. Thorne's team members had obviously learned the art of not showing any emotions. If Priest considered Thorne a friend, that didn't show on his face. Raine thought the whole team creepily detached, considering they were here to kill their leader.

Raine had faced death many times. In the past, his life had always been the only one on the line. Now he feared for Thorne more than he did for himself. Clutching him tighter, he growled warningly.

Lance's eyebrow hiked up and his lips curled in clear amusement. "Got yourself a pet, commander? Cute."

Thorne fired a shot into the ground close to Lance's feet. "Watch your mouth. Next shot is to your balls."

Lance didn't so much as flinch.

"You're in no position to threaten us," Cross said with cold fury. He came closer, gun raised at Thorne's head. "You betrayed us."

Raine tried to crawl around and over Thorne to shield him with his body.

Thorne wouldn't let him and pinned him underneath his

heavier body.

"He's going to shoot you!" Raine pushed and pulled, growing desperate.

"We'll die anyway." Thorne's voice was so damn calm.

"How can you be so . . ." Raine struggled free. He stood and turned, glaring at Cross. "And you! How dare you act all haughty and righteous? You're assassins. Not exactly the moral pillars of society."

"Shh." Thorne struggled to his feet, wobbled, and pulled Raine against his chest. His whole body tensed when Priest pushed Cross to the side and came to a stop in front of them.

Priest studied them like bugs under a magnifying glass. Slowly, deliberately, he slid a terrifyingly big knife from a sheath at his hip.

Raine swallowed and slid in front of Thorne. "Fine. Bring it on. Thorne, you better start shooting." He didn't understand why Thorne hadn't dished out some bullets already. Okay, they were his team members. But they obviously didn't mind shooting him.

When Priest took a step toward Raine, Thorne's arm curled around him from behind. Thorne raised his arm and pointed the gun at Priest's chest. Raine felt him take a deep breath.

Priest must've seen something in Thorne's gaze, because his eyes widened and his mouth fell open. "Are you fucking serious?"

"We saw you snogging, but I didn't think you'd choose him over us." Lance sounded offended.

Raine huffed. "Of course he's choosing me. I'm not the one trying to kill him."

"Cross Shepherd, don't even think about it," Thorne warned.

Raine hadn't noticed the blond inching toward them.

Thorne shuffled them back, swinging the gun in an arch toward his team.

"Why?" Priest asked flatly.

Thorne growled. "Because he's my mate."

Raine's breath caught, watching for the men's reaction.

While Lance cursed and rubbed a hand through his black hair, Priest's face distorted with anger. And Cross? His finger twitched on the trigger.

Wait. "Cross Shepherd?" Raine's mind raced. He made himself a broader target in front of Thorne. "Related to Aaron Shepherd?"

Priest's reaction was fast as lightning. He raised his arm, closed his hand around Cross's wrist, and pushed his hand up.

Thorne tackled Raine to the ground. A shot echoed in Raine's ears. The bullet whizzed through the air. Leaves, twigs, and more droplets rained down on them. A couple of birds screeched and flapped. Then silence.

Slowly, carefully, Raine raised his head from under Thorne's arm.

Cross was pale. He didn't fight when Priest peeled the gun from his fingers. "What do you know about Aaron?"

Narrowing his eyes, Raine dipped into his training and took a calming breath. "I know that if you ever want to see your little brother again, you'll keep your overly nervous trigger finger in check."

Cross snarled and tensed, readying to charge at them.

Priest pushed him back. "Calm the fuck down." He fixed his gaze on Raine. "Where's the kid?"

"Safe." Raine met Thorne's puzzled gaze. "I promise. Us rebels don't tend to torture children. A recon team found him at one of the labs." He paused, then focused back on Cross. "Close to starving, according to the report I read."

Cross' face crumbled. "I knew it. I fucking knew it." He shook off Lance when the other assassin tried to comfort him. "I should never have left him alone! I'm a sorry excuse for a—

"

"Stop whining." A man dressed in greens and browns, with twigs and leaves sticking from his outfit, joined the group. He had a sniper rifle slung over his shoulder. "You made a deal with the devil, Cross. Not once, but twice. We all did." His green-eyed gaze slid over Thorne and Raine. "Commander found himself a mate, huh? Can we stop pretending to kill him and deal with it?" He placed his hands on his hips. "Commander, you should get up. Seeing you rolling on the ground is, frankly, pathetic. I only shot you in the leg."

Lance chuckled. "Right? I remember when Priest and the commander had a disagreement and Priest stabbed him. Nicked his kidney. He didn't act like a baby back then."

"He stabbed you over a disagreement?" Raine helped Thorne up.

Thorne slung one arm over Raine's shoulders and glared at Priest. "Yeah. Suddenly there was a fifth ace in that deck of cards."

"Wait." Raine pressed his hand against Thorne's heaving chest. "He stabbed you in the kidney over a poker game?"

"Commander's always way too serious." Priest shrugged. "And I patched him right up. I bet he's a whiney baby because he's found someone to coddle him. Let's return to the car and check your leg."

"No." Raine frowned. "Minutes ago, you wanted to kill us both. We're going nowhere with you." The whole situation was beyond fucked-up. Were they still planning to off them? Or were they on his and Thorne's side because Raine knew where Aaron was?

Lance hooted. "Woohoo. The commander's man is fierce and protective."

"Shut up, Lance." The sniper cuffed him upside the head then focused on Raine. "Name's Kee Bishop, by the way. Welcome to the family." He winked at Thorne. "Nice Christmas sweater, commander. Dancing reindeer on a red background made following you through my scope easy as fuck."

Thorne growled.

Priest raised his hands. "To make this clear, we were trying to find you before the other team did. When we saw you smooching a shifter . . ." He sneered. "Let's just say Kee wasn't too happy. We thought you had switched sides." Priest's gaze was solemn. "You . . . haven't switched sides. Right?"

Thorne sighed deeply.

When Raine looked up at him, he saw the conflict on his mate's face. He was afraid Thorne's answer wouldn't go over well with his team. Raine braced himself for more bullets to fly their way.

Thorne gazed at the men he'd—aside from Cross—suffered, trained, joked, and lived with for the past decade. Cross had joined the team two years ago, after they'd lost Pierce Rosenkrans to one of Taylor's debriefings. The experience should've pushed them closer together. Instead Thorne had pulled away, afraid to lose another part of his makeshift family.

He met Priest's gaze calmly. Priest was the brother he'd never had. Having to choose between him and Raine was . . . it felt like a knife to his kidney. He smirked. "My man's one of the rebels. Tried to convince him to run away with me. When we talked on the phone, you knew I wouldn't come back. Right?"

Priest's shoulders slumped. "Yeah." He closed the distance and sank to his knee, reaching for Thorne's leg. "After Pierce . . . yeah. And Taylor knows we'd rather die than kill you."

Something finally registered. "Wait. You said *before the*

other team found us." Thorne leaned onto Raine while he allowed Priest to check the bullet wound. "He didn't send you guys. What are you doing here?"

"Guess, asshole." Kee rolled his eyes. "Saving your hide. And your man's. When Priest was worried you'd switched sides, it had nothing to do with you turning your back on Taylor. We don't fucking care about that asswipe's hurt feelings or anything."

"Can we trust them?" Raine muttered.

Thorne brushed a kiss over Raine's temple. "We don't have another choice. They're as dead as we are if the other team finds us. They went against Taylor's orders."

"Aww, aren't they the sweetest cupcakes?" Lance grinned while he leaned casually against Kee's side, only to giggle when Kee pushed him away. "Brute." He blew Kee a kiss.

Thorne ignored their antics and concentrated on Priest. "Raine asked me—without actually asking me—to help him and his boss to kick Thoreau's ass." He waited until Priest looked up from where he bandaged Thorne's leg. "Are you in?" Thorne was asking a lot. His team might die if they followed him.

"Wait." Raine grabbed his chin and turned his head. "When did you decide to help me? I thought you wanted to remain . . . impartial. You said you're not interested in shifter politics."

Thorne stole a quick kiss. "Well, that decision flew out the window last night, don't you think? We're bonded. I might be a bastard of epic proportions, but I know what bonding means to a shifter. And—" he lowered his voice "—I think it might mean as much to me."

Raine blinked. "That soothes my worries about whether or not I can trust you unconditionally."

"Fuck, Wilder." Priest's sigh was long and suffering. "I never felt as loyal to Thoreau as you anyway. I stayed with the team so you and these yahoos wouldn't die. Of course I'm with you." He stood and offered Raine his hand. "Priest Cavendish. Nice to meet you."

Raine shook his hand with a suspicious glare. Clever mate.

Cross stepped forward. "Taylor used my brother against me. I'm in."

"He killed Pierce," Lance whispered, reaching for Kee.

Kee sighed and brushed Lance's hand away. "You're as good as dead without me. And you're the only people I can tolerate without killing them or causing them unimaginable pain. Count me in."

Priest slapped Thorne's shoulder. "We were pissed because we thought you'd abandoned us, asshole. When you called, I was prepared to pack up and pick you up wherever. But you hung up without so much as a goodbye." He pushed up into Thorne's face, his dark eyes blazing. "*No*body abandons me."

Right. He should've thought of Priest's fucking abandonment issues. Thorne pulled Priest into a quick manly hug, letting him go when Raine growled.

"Down, tiger." Priest raised an eyebrow. "Mr. Celibate is all yours. I prefer my men *with* a sex drive. Anyway, I'd never fuck a guy who's as close to me as a brother."

"You should try it sometime." Lance yelped when Kee slapped the back of his head again. "What?" He raised his hands and grinned.

Thorne rolled his eyes. He'd been waiting for these two to get their shit together for years. No such luck. He shook his head when Raine opened his mouth. Thorne pressed a quick kiss to Raine's lush lips, smiling when Raine immediately returned the kiss, not caring about the onlookers.

Priest chuckled. "Happy and in lurve suits you, commander. But let's ditch the forest. Damn fog gives me fucking depression."

Thorne ended the kiss. In love? Nah. It was way too soon to think of love. And Thorne wasn't one for mushy feelings. But he saw the blush on Raine's cheeks and thought that, if they were still alive tomorrow, he wouldn't mind mushiness.

Chapter Nine

Raine's head was spinning with the turn of events. He sat beside Thorne, who had a possessive arm around his shoulders, in the back seat of an SUV packed to the roof with deadly assassins with even deadlier fangs.

Priest was driving, quietly talking with Kee, who sat beside him on the passenger seat reading a map. Thorne had made sure his team didn't carry any electronic gizmos that allowed tracking before they took off.

Lance and Cross sat in front of them. While Lance kept annoying Kee by blowing against his neck and flicking his ear, Cross had turned and was staring at them.

"What can you tell me about my baby brother? Is he okay?"

Raine sighed. "Not much, honestly. I thought mentioning him would keep you from putting a bullet between our eyes." He shrugged. "Before Thorne invited me on a cross-country trip, my boss got a report from Alpha Xander Powell. Two of his men found Aaron in a lab close to the Canadian border. Already turned. He's well cared for. I bet he's missing you. How old is he?"

"Seventeen." Cross lowered his gaze. He ran his index finger along the seam of the leather seat. "Maybe he wants to see me. Maybe not. He might hate me. I arranged for Taylor to treat him. Because . . . I'm selfish. I didn't want to lose him. He's very sick. *Was* sick."

Lance granted a grumpy Kee a reprieve from his teasing and touched Cross' arm. "You had the best intentions. He would've died without the treatment."

"Yeah. And now my baby brother is a monster. Like me," Cross snapped.

Raine felt Thorne tense beside him. He knew his mate thought of himself as a monster as well. Raine rubbed Thorne's chest in circles. "You're not. Are you an upstanding citizen? No. But neither am I. I'm a Council spy and interrogator. I kill and torture people as well." He smiled when Thorne kissed his temple.

Cross and Lance both watched them, one curious, the other with longing.

"This is so weird," Cross whispered. "The commander is never . . . gentle." He said the word as though weighing it on his tongue. "Is that the mate bond?" He frowned. "Wait . . . is there a mate waiting for all of us?" Poor Cross paled.

Raine shrugged. "Who knows? It's not unusual for a shifter to find their mate in a human. The human usually experiences the mating pull as strong attraction, while shifters rely on scent to recognize their one and only. Anyway, you're not fully human anymore."

"Yeah." Lance scratched the bridge of his nose. "When Taylor fiddled with our DNA and added shifter juice to the mix . . ." His eyes widened. "Thorne, how did you know Raine was yours?"

Thorne grinned. "He made my dick hard." He grunted when Raine elbowed him.

Cross smirked. "That's pretty amazing, Raine. The commander's indifference when it comes to hook-ups has been a running joke for the team."

Raine sighed, not pleased about the team making fun of his mate's issues. He'd never in a million years expected them to be jokesters, either. "Thorne learned I was his mate because I slipped up and told him."

"That's not exactly correct," Thorne murmured. He met Raine's gaze and brushed a lock of hair from Raine's forehead. "You carry the most amazing scent. I chalked it up to being close to starving, thought it was your blood calling me to you. But your freshly-mown grass scent is . . . it reminds me of my past."

Lance raised his hand like a schoolboy, interrupting their heart-to-heart. "So you're horny for Raine and want to sniff and lick him all the time?"

Kee coughed in the front seat, folding the map loudly. "Discussing the commander's love life has to wait. We don't have a plan yet for joining Raine's rebel buddies. They might shoot us on sight. I know what I'd do if the enemy came to my house."

Raine glanced out the window, suddenly realizing where they were going. "Are you insane? You can't roll up to Alpha Xander's house like you were invited for afternoon tea." He turned to Thorne and fisted his sweater. "Kee's right. Tell them to stop the car. Priest, stop the fucking car. We need a plan. Xander's enforcers will strike first and ask questions later. They've already been attacked by assassins once. The alpha has increased patrols because of that." Stupid, reckless, cocky assassins, thinking they were invincible.

Surprisingly, Priest actually slowed the vehicle and pulled off to the side of the road leading right to Wildcat Hills Pride territory. He turned in his seat. "I hear Powell's a reasonable guy. Way more chill than Alpha Haas, anyway. And Powell is, according to our intel, leader of the rebels. If we want to offer our services, we'd better bend over for the head honcho, right?" He smirked.

Raine ran a hand through his hair. "Xander Powell also has a tiny mate and three grand-babies he protects fiercely." He pursed his lips. "If I had a phone, I'd call Bailey and tell him to—"

"Bailey?" Kee turned as well, pinning Raine with his green-eyed gaze. "Doctor Bailey Atherton?"

Thorne groaned. "Right. I forgot about noble Doctor Conscience. He's in Wildcat Hills, is he? I thought he belonged to Haas' men."

Raine nodded. "Yean, he's here. I'm guessing you don't care much for him?" He'd had the same feeling when he'd mentioned Bailey during the interrogation. Raine watched Thorne cross his arms over his chest, stubbornness visible on his face.

Lance cackled. "They hate each other. Bailey never got used to killing for Thoreau, and his self-hatred grew with every mission. Thorne always thought he was weak and named him Doctor Conscience as an insult."

"Shut it," Thorne snarled. "I did no such thing. I voted for Doctor Dick."

Raine ignored his mate. "The pride calls him Doctor Fang. Not everyone at the pride is happy with him residing in Wildcat Hills, but he's respected as a doctor. And he saved Thorne's life after London shot him."

Kee smirked. "Nice. Now you owe him, commander. He might put in a good word for us with the cats, too. If you can stop yourself from stabbing him."

"Nobody will stab anyone once we reach the pride." Raine jumped in his seat when a siren sounded behind them. "What . . ." He turned and, seeing the blue light, cursed. "Really? A patrol car?"

"It's a sheriff's vehicle," Kee mumbled.

Raine suddenly remembered the Chief of the Green Valley police department being a cat shifter. "Fuck. Either Xander knows we're in his territory, or he will know in a couple of minutes." Raine shot the men in the car warning looks. "Act normal and non-threatening." He took note of the knives strapped to Priest, and the gun in Cross's hand. Kee was growling, his eyes a deep red color that freaked Raine out more than a little. And Lance showed his fangs while cracking his knuckles. "Forget normal. But no attacking the cop. Or snacking on him," he said with a glare toward Kee.

Kee merely smirked.

"Damn, he's hot," Cross whispered.

Raine focused on the cop. His uniform was black, with a star pinned to one side of his chest and a name tag to the other. "Shit. That hottie is the chief himself." He didn't remember his name. The man drew closer to the car with a relaxed swagger, but he had one hand on the butt of his gun. "Lower the window, Priest."

"I love a silver daddy." Cross hummed.

Thorne slapped his head from behind. "My mate said no snacking."

Raine understood where Cross was coming from. The chief had salt-and-pepper hair and a matching short beard. He stood roughly six feet, with a wide chest and muscled arms. His belly wasn't flat, but softly rounded. Raine guessed the cuddliness added to his daddy appeal.

The chief stopped beside the car the moment Priest lowered the window. He took a peek into the car and dipped his head. "Gentlemen. Driver's license and vehicle documentation, please." He met Raine's gaze with calm strength.

Raine checked his name tag. *Right. Hunter Sterling. Caracal shifter.* He'd planned to increase CCTV around the area with Romeo's help shortly before Raine and Armand had left the pride. Was he aware at least five of the six men in the car were able to kill him in thirty different ways with nothing but a paper clip? If he was, his face and scent gave nothing away. *Cool as a cucumber.*

"Nope, sorry." Priest shrugged his wide shoulders. "Must've forgotten them in my other car."

"Get out of the vehicle, please." The chief took a step back and placed both hands on his hips.

Kee leaned over Priest. "All of us, sir?"

Raine squeezed Thorne's hand, leaned over him, and

grabbed for the door handle.

"Where the fuck do you think you're going?" Thorne snarled.

"Preventing a blood bath." Raine shrugged off Thorne's hands, crawled over him, and slipped from the car. "Chief Sterling." He held up his hands in a non-threatening way. "These men are with me. They're not here to cause any harm . . . to the pride," he added when Sterling's eyebrows rose up to his hairline. "Look, one of them's my mate."

Sterling pursed his lips. "Raine Cosworth?"

"Yes."

The chief lifted his hand to the mic on his shoulder. "Dispatch. I found the car. Passengers are fine. Lost tourists struggling with how to read a map. I'll send them on their way and go on my break."

The mic crackled. Raine heard the dispatcher reply with, "Ten-four, chief."

Sterling held out his hand. "Mr. Cosworth, we were worried about you.

Raine shook the proffered hand with a relieved smile.

Sterling retrieved his phone from his belt. "I'm calling the alpha. One wrong move from your friends and we'll add some nice bullet holes to your shiny new SUV. Got me, son?"

Raine nodded quickly as he gazed around the area. How had he missed the signs? Worry for his mate must truly fuck with his concentration.

Sterling dipped his head. "And tell surfer boy to stop looking at me like I'm a snack, or I'll pull out his fangs and wear them as a necklace."

True enough, Cross's face was pressed to the window as he drooled over the chief. Raine rolled his eyes, slapping his hand against the glass. "He'll behave. It's not your vein he's after. At least . . . it's not *only* your vein he wants to suck."

Sterling scoffed and took a couple of steps from the car.

Raine leaned down and met Priest's gaze. "Guess the pride got their own sharpshooters. Don't do anything rash. If Thorne gets hurt because one of you fucks up, you'll learn what a shifter is capable of when his mate's in danger."

Priest gave him a two-finger-salute. "You're the boss, commate."

"Get it?" Lance leaned through the gap between Kee and Priest's seats and looked at Raine. "That's short for the commander's—"

Kee pressed his whole palm over Lance's face and shoved him back into his seat. "He gets it, pest."

Raine turned when Sterling nudged him. He took the cell the chief offered him and lifted it to his ear. "Yes?"

"Two questions. Which of the assassins is your mate and do you trust him?"

Raine rubbed his forehead with his thumb and index finger. Xander asking questions was a good sign, right? "It's Wilder. And yes. With my life. I'd appreciate it if you didn't kill us." He met his mate's gaze through the window, smiling slightly at Thorne's petulant expression. Raine knew Thorne heard every word he said, and probably Xander's as well thanks to his advanced senses.

Xander's deep sigh sounded through the line. "I'll probably regret this. But I'll hear what you have to say." The line disconnected.

Raine handed the cell back to Sterling, who pocketed it.

"I'll accompany you to Xander's so you won't be blown to smithereens as soon as you enter the village."

Raine choked. "Wait . . . blown up? What the hell?" The pride sure had used the last couple of days to beef up security.

Sterling nodded. "Beta Alan went a touch overboard. On the other hand, he has reason—his pregnant sister's moved to Wildcat Hills until the delivery, since she's acting as surrogate for Alan and his mate."

Raine nodded. "Okay." Where the hell had Alan gotten the equipment to blow up a vehicle?

Sterling obviously picked up on his helplessness and chuckled. He pointed at the car. "Are you sure your guests are on the up-and-up?"

"My mate's on our side. And his team is a hundred percent loyal to him." Raine didn't feel as sure as he pretended. But he'd always been good at bullshitting others. There was only one way to find out if Thorne's merry gang of psychopaths would keep their word.

Chapter Ten

Thorne was proud of Raine. It probably wasn't easy to trust men—assassins—he'd met for the first time only a couple of hours ago. Or him, for that matter. Raine had to know he was risking the safety of the pride by bringing Thorne's team to Wildcat Hills. Thorne would personally skin any of his men who caused a pride member harm. His mate's trust had become the most important thing to him, and he wouldn't allow anyone—not even his brothers-in-arms—to fuck it up.

Priest slowed the car to a stop in the middle of a village square.

Cute houses in different colors, with cuter porches and porch swings, surrounded the square on three sides. The fog hadn't followed them from the woods, and the sun peeking from behind the clouds from time to time gave everything an idyllic tinge.

Well, if it weren't for the heavily armed men slowly leaving the porches and walking toward their car. Thorne tightened his hold on Raine's hand. He hoped Chief Sterling hadn't bullshitted them. His men were excellent fighters. But they wouldn't survive a blaze of gunfire.

Chief Sterling exited his cruiser and waved. "Awful weather we've had lately, huh? It's supposed to snow pretty soon." He tapped his nose. "I can smell it."

Thorne thought the chief's attempt at casual chit-chat pretty surreal.

"Commander, are these dudes holding bows?" Lance asked, amusement coloring his voice.

Thorne wasn't surprised. Most situations amused Lance. Sure enough, two men who flanked a tall, white-blond haired man held bows, their arrows ready to fly and cause a nasty wound. Thorne himself had been hit by an arrow twice and wasn't looking forward to experiencing it again.

Raine leaned forward between the seats. "The Native American is enforcer Jaxon. The African American is Xander's son-in-law Djimon. The latter is a sleep-deprived father of triplets, so don't make him angry."

Thorne recognized Xander Powell from the file he'd read on him and the pride. The white lion shifter was a force of nature. An ex-soldier, too. Thorne saw Beta Alan holding an old-fashioned rifle, while enforcer Finley was armed with a machine gun. *Nice.*

The only unarmed enforcer was Malcolm. Although, as a tiger shifter, he didn't necessarily need a gun to kill them. The big red-head stood close to a man Thorne had hoped to never see again.

"Atherton," he pressed out between his teeth. The guy had always rubbed him the wrong way. And not just because he made Thorne feel as though fulfilling his duty meant he was evil incarnate.

Raine sighed. "At least try to remain civil. I'm sure Doctor Fang will want to have a look at your leg. Out of the car, guys. We're making them nervous."

Kee snorted. "*We* are making *them* nervous? I'm not the one playing with the big guns. Yet." Still, he was the first to open the door, raise his hands, and exit the car.

One after another they left the vehicle and pooled beside it. Thorne couldn't help himself and moved his body half in front of Raine.

His mate sighed exasperatedly and muttered, "I'm not the one in danger."

"We're not playing." Xander came down the porch steps,

head held high and back straight. "We've seen you guys in action. If this is a trap . . ."

"It's not." Raine slipped around Thorne and positioned himself in front of the team.

"Mate." Thorne snarled and prowled after him. Before he managed to grab him, he heard the unmistakable noise of a bowstring tightening. A scar on his back began to prickle. He lifted his hands. "Dammit. I'm not a threat to my own mate."

Xander's ice blue eyes narrowed. "Step away from him."

Thorne bit his tongue. It went against every protective—and possessive—instinct he had, but he did as Xander said. He nodded at a worried-looking Raine, trying to convey that he had himself under control.

Raine approached Xander, his hand held out. "Alpha, thank you for giving us a chance to explain ourselves."

"I don't like this," Kee muttered under his breath, gazing around furtively.

Thorne agreed with him. Unease slithered through him when he watched Xander take Raine's hand. Apart from not liking a powerful male touching his mate, Thorne had a weird feeling of foreboding.

Xander narrowed his eyes and dipped his head, his gaze fixed on the side of Raine's neck. Fast as lightning, Xander yanked Raine around and pressed Raine's back against his chest. Before Thorne realized what was happening, Xander had pressed a small knife to Raine's neck.

"No!" Thorne wanted to tackle the alpha and free his mate, but Priest's hand on his shoulder stopped him. Thorne snarled at his second-in-command. When Priest dipped his head, Thorne swung around and discovered two arrows trained on him. *Fuck.* "What the hell? Raine said you were trustworthy." He searched Xander's gaze, but those cool eyes gave nothing away.

Raine was panting harshly, his hands wrapped around

Xander's arm where it rested over his upper chest. "Sir . . . Alpha . . ." He swallowed. "Thorne, don't do anything rash."

Thorne growled.

"I'd listen to the man you claim is your mate," Xander said calmly.

"Claim? He *is* my mate. And if you hurt a hair on his head, I'll end you." Thorne's pulse raced. He flicked his gaze back and forth between the bowmen and Xander, wondering where the bows would hit him and whether he'd still manage to reach his mate before he hit the ground.

Raine made a distressed sound. "Don't. Please. I heard Djimon is an exceptional archer. He . . . won't miss his mark."

Thorne raised his hands palm up. When Kee twitched, his hand going to his waist, he hissed. "Stop. Don't move a muscle." He focused on Xander. "What will it take for you to take the knife from my man's throat? Tell me and I'll do it. Anything." He sounded desperate, but fuck it. The fear and confusion in Raine's eyes tugged at his dead black heart.

It was Alan who answered. "You'll take off you weapons. All of them."

"Oh man." Cross sighed. "That might take a couple of hours." He turned to Chief Sterling. "Wanna frisk me, hot stuff?"

Thorne growled. "Stop thinking with your dick for once in your life and take off your weapons." Keeping his right arm raised, he slowly reached for his gun with the left. "I'm right-handed, okay? Don't hurt him."

Raine shivered in Xander's hold. "I understand you don't trust us, but I never thought—"

"The last time I had an assassin in my house, I almost lost my son and grand-children." Xander snorted. "And the whole mate business between you two is too convenient. How do I know you haven't been turned and are now working for the enemy?"

Thorne had to admit Xander was a smart leader. "Weapons, guys." If a bunch of armed men who'd once tried to kill him suddenly claimed they wanted to help, he'd be suspicious as fuck, too. But while he somehow admired Xander's ballsy move, the beast inside him wanted to rip the alpha's throat out for threatening their man.

Slowly, Thorne's teammates began to pile their weapons—guns, knives, grenades, brass knuckles, slingshots, and throwing stars—on the ground.

Raine patted Xander's arm. "No, it's true. We claimed each other last night. Thorne would never hurt me by . . ." He trailed off when Xander pressed the knife harder against his neck.

"Hey." Thorne took a step forward. "What else do you want? You can restrain me. Every one of us, for all I care." He lowered to his knees in the dirt, holding Raine's gaze. "It's okay, Red."

"Commander." Kee sounded pissed. "You'd risk us being completely vulnerable to save your—"

"Shut it." Thorne showed Kee his fangs. "I'd do anything for him. You'd understand it if you pulled your head out of your ass and faced the truth for once." That was a low blow toward his friend. But Thorne didn't have time to cater to hurt feelings.

Kee lifted his hands up high, a dangerous glimmer in his eyes as he stepped away from his pile of arms. While doing so, he inched in front of Lance. "Fine."

Thorne turned when he heard a relieved sigh. Xander had let Raine go. Thorne stood quickly and slung his arms around his mate. "Fuck."

"Yeah." Raine ran both hands over the back of his head and his nape. "Thank you for not going on a killing spree."

"Wasn't easy." Thorne caught Raine's lips in a quick and dirty kiss, then met Xander's gaze. "Happy?"

Xander arched an eyebrow. "Congrats on your mating. I had to be sure." He returned the knife to somewhere behind his back. "I want to know what the hell happened at Donavan's. Don't you dare lie to me."

Raine swallowed around a lump the size of one of the grenades Kee had had strapped to his body. Still shaken from feeling cold steel against his neck, he drew strength from Thorne's closeness.

"In honor of your offer to listen to me, I'll tell you the truth and say that Thorne Wilder used my weakness for him to escape. And he'll claim that he took me with him as a hostage. Truth is, he knew I was his mate. He never hurt me. He offered to leave the country with me so we'd be safe from his team and Thoreau's wrath." Raine waved a hand at the men, wincing when he saw them scowl. "We're here together because . . . I refused to leave you hanging."

Xander arched one white-blond brow. "Another one bites the dust, huh?" He focused on Thorne's team and regarded them with suspicion. "And you brought more killers to my home why?"

Raine followed his gaze and suppressed a groan. Stupid Kee still had his hands raised high in the air and he grinned. Cross kept staring at the Chief and had moved closer to him without anyone noticing. Or at least without anyone shooting him. Priest looked torn between throwing himself in front of Thorne—out of duty—or Raine—to please his commander—if things went downhill. And Lance was hiding halfway behind Kee and thought nobody saw him playing with a big-ass knife he should've thrown down earlier.

Xander was obviously aware of Lance's toy, because he glared and opened his mouth. But before he had the chance to demand Lance part with his plaything, a door to one of the houses on Raine's right was yanked open.

A high-pitched squeal sounded, followed by hurried steps. Raine saw a slender figure streak across the square, long blond hair flowing in the wind. The person was too fast to be anything but another altered human.

"Cross!"

"Aaron, no!" Vaughn Christian came barreling down the porch steps, running after the young man.

Raine's eyes widened when realization hit home. The reunion of the brothers might very well turn into a disaster. With Vaughn hurrying after Aaron without regards for his own safety, enforcer Finley abandoned his gun and ran toward his mate.

Cross finally tore his gaze from the chief and turned. A wide grin split his face as he opened his arms wide, waiting for Aaron to fly into them. But instead of Aaron's slight body hitting Cross' in a hug, Cross was tackled from behind by a snarling Sterling.

"What the actual fuck?" Priest shouted and marched toward the tussling men.

Xander stopped Priest with a hand on his chest.

Although Priest snarled and clenched his fists, he didn't force his way past Xander. "Do something. Cross hasn't seen his brother in close to six months. He doesn't pose a danger to Aaron. There's no need for the cop to intervene."

Aaron came to a sudden stop in front of his brother and Sterling. "Please, let him go."

"It's fine." Vaughn came up behind Aaron and looped his arm around his waist.

"It's not." Aaron stomped his foot. "I want to hug my brother. Chief, please."

Raine watched Sterling tense at Aaron's words. He had his arm slung around Cross' neck from behind and sat on the man's ass.

Cross, despite struggling for breath, waved at Aaron and grinned. "Hey, bro. Give me a sec to deal with Chief Snuggles. He's obviously too jealous to let me hug you. I felt serious vibes between us earlier." Cross patted Sterling's arm where it rested across his windpipe. "Sugar, can we postpone the foreplay until I've checked on my brother?"

Sterling growled low in his throat and tightened his hold for a second. Then he got up, pushing Cross's head down. "Stop flirting with me. You couldn't handle me anyway." Sterling dusted off his uniform and stepped around a chuckling Cross. "I'm sorry for . . . inconveniencing your brother, little one. I doubt I hurt him. It's good to see you again."

"Chief Sterling." A soft blush spread over Aaron's cheeks as he took Sterling's offered hand.

"Hunter. Please."

The blush on Aaron's cheeks deepened. "My brother always had a hard head. No offence taken." He peeked around Sterling. "Do you plan on getting up anytime soon, Cross? I see you still know how to charm men into getting a restraining order against you."

Cross rolled to his feet gracefully. He pulled Aaron from Sterling's hold and enfolded him in a bear hug. "I missed you so much, little bug." Cross closed his eyes and nuzzled between Aaron's long hair, breathing him in. "How are you?" He pushed Aaron an arms' length away and looked him over. "Your cheeks are rosy and your eyes are shining. Are you in pain? Thirsty?"

Aaron giggled. "I'm fine. Let me introduce you to my foster dads." He waved at a fidgety Vaughn and a smiling Finley. "Fin, Vaughn, meet my older brother Cross."

"Foster what now?"

Raine snorted at Cross' incredulous expression. He turned his back on the family reunion and focused on Thorne. His mate was involved in a staring battle with Xander and Beta

Alan. "Babe." He was pleased when Thorne immediately wrapped his arm around him.

Alan chuckled. "Glad to see you alive and kicking. Thought you'd end up as a quick nibble for assassin boy. I owe Djimon fifty bugs."

"Yes, well." Xander cleared his throat. "Good that my very concerned-for-your-health second-in-command was wrong. Please excuse me for forcing you to stay in the cold this time of the year, but I have family."

"Bet you have no problem with him being inside your home." Thorne dipped his chin toward a hovering Bailey.

Bailey must've heard, because he raised one eyebrow. "I didn't kidnap a council employee to snack on him either."

"Nope. You snacked on Alpha Haas' mate," Thorne shot back. "Heard it through the grapevine."

Bailey snarled. "Remind me again why I saved your life when London shot you?"

"Because you've always been a bleeding heart, Doctor Dick."

"I'll show you the meaning of bleeding heart, asshole." Bailey started forward but was yanked back by Malcolm. "Mal, give me your stake."

Malcolm laughed. "What would I need a stake for?"

"You said you carry one."

"To yank your chain." Malcolm tightened his hold around Bailey's arm.

Bailey palmed his face and focused on Thorne. "Let's agree to avoid each other while you're Xander's guest."

"Enough," Xander said with calm strength. "Avoiding each other won't be possible if Thorne decides to join our cause." He pursed his lips, snapped his fingers, and pointed to where the team had left their weapons. Several pride members hurried over and collected them. "Are you joining our cause, or did you come to ask for Raine's hand and whisk him off to Greenland?"

Thorne laughed. "I had considered that. But Raine would stake me himself if I forced him to leave the country. I'm . . . offering my service in your fight against Thoreau. I'll tell you the name of our last mark. The mission was called off, but she might still be in danger."

Raine knew uttering those words wasn't easy for Thorne.

Xander scratched his chin. "And your men?"

"They signed their own death sentences by following me." Thorne rubbed his hand over his bald head. "Thoreau sent a team to kill me. My men left base to rescue me. That's a betrayal punishable by death."

"No second chances for assassins, hm?" Xander placed his hands on his hips and took a harsh breath. "They'll join you in battle if necessary?"

Raine watched Thorne place his hand over his heart.

"Yes. You have my word. No harm will come to the pride by my men's hands, or I'll discipline them myself." Thorne looked torn for a second. "Still . . . they need food."

Obviously, Xander knew what Thorne meant. "I have a standing order for Bailey. I'll stock up on it." The warning was clear in his voice. *Don't snack on anyone.*

Raine shifted nervously. "The bite isn't as bad as I thought. I guess it depends on the intention. And the connection between both parties involved."

Bailey tensed and Malcolm rubbed his neck, but Raine dismissed their behavior. He huddled closer to Thorne when a gust of wind hit him and blew his hair into his eyes. He brushed it away. "Can we go somewhere warm? My balls are freezing off." Raine smiled when Thorne rubbed his back. "My mate is also injured and needs to rest."

Malcolm came forward. "My house?"

"Yes. First, I need the name, Thorne."

"Alpha Hollister."

Xander raised his hand and twirled his index finger through the air. "Alan and Jaxon will go with you." He hesitated for a second. "Bailey as well. Try not to stake each other," he said with a stern look for the doctor.

Bailey grunted. "Since Malcolm lied to me about having a supply of stakes at home, my hands are tied."

Malcolm laughed. He slung an arm around Bailey and steered him away from Xander. "Just because I said I don't carry a stake doesn't mean I don't have some stashed away in my wine cellar."

Raine followed the odd pair with Thorne close by his side, supporting him.

Bailey shot them an exasperated look over his shoulder. "Malcolm doesn't have a wine cellar. Asshole doesn't know the difference between Merlot and Chardonnay."

"And?" Malcolm sounded disgruntled. "I'm not a wine expert. Who the hell can tell the varieties apart?"

"Really, Mal?" Priest said dryly. "One's red and the other white. You don't have to be a sommelier to discern which is which."

Malcolm turned and frowned. "What did you call me?"

Kee chuckled behind Raine and muttered, "Hell. At least he's pretty and buff, huh?"

Chapter Eleven

If someone had asked Thorne how he imagined a meeting between his team and a heavily armed group of shifters who considered them their enemies would play out, this scenario would not have made it on the top ten list of possibilities.

Thorne sat on a gray-and-green striped sofa in a way-too-cute living room, holding a delicate porcelain cup of coffee. An étagère sat in the middle of the coffee table, displaying tiny cucumber sandwiches and shortbread. A fucking étagère.

If his leg wasn't throbbing like hell, he'd think this was a dream.

From the look of disbelief on Raine's face, Thorne guessed his mate was equally confused.

His team seemed divided. Lance was comfortable enough to stuff his face with sandwiches. Give him food and he was happy.

Kee, though, had surprised Thorne by lifting his pinky finger when he'd taken a careful sip from his teacup. Fucking traitor looked like he'd been brought up on tea, nibbles, and polite chit-chat, as he was currently immersed in a bow-hunting conversation with Jaxon.

Priest leaned back in an armchair, arms crossed over his chest while he scowled at the food and tea as though Malcolm was trying to poison them. And poor Cross seemed torn between following his idol's example and grabbing a cookie.

Raine sighed, leaned forward, and picked up a cookie. He

tossed it toward Cross, who snatched it and engulfed the whole thing in one bite.

Priest gave Raine a chiding look.

"Calm down, Cavendish." Bailey circled a spoon through his cup lazily. The sound grated on Thorne's nerves. "We didn't poison the cookies. It's in the sandwiches."

Lance's eyes widened briefly. His cheeks were puffed out while he chewed.

Kee snorted. "He's bluffing. I saw Malcolm eat a sandwich while he prepared them in the kitchen."

Suddenly Malcolm started coughing. He raised both hands to his throat while he started wheezing and shaking.

Raine yelled and jumped to his feet. "What the—"

Thorne grabbed the back of Raine's sweater before he was able to rush over to the tiger shifter.

Malcolm's tongue lolled from his mouth. He slid from the love seat he'd sat on beside Bailey and tumbled to the floor.

Oddly enough, Bailey merely rolled his eyes.

"The fuck?" Thorne snarled.

Every eye in the room turned on him, then back to Malcolm. The man lay still for a second, tongue hanging out and eyes crossed. After a moment of complete silence, he started giggling and holding his belly. He tried to roll away when Bailey nudged Malcolm's side with his socked foot. "No poking the dead!"

"I'll poke you with a stake if you don't cease this behavior at once." Bailey shook his head and sniffed, but the side of his mouth curled up. "God, you're such a dork." He started laughing.

Raine sat back down beside Thorne and leaned closer.

Lance snapped up another sandwich, and even Priest couldn't contain a chuckle.

Thorne threw an arm around his mate and growled. "Assholes. Both of you." Though he had to admit, Bailey and

Malcolm's joke had drained the tension from the room.

Raine kissed his cheek. "It's not easy to poison a shifter, because our sense of smell is outstanding."

"Ours as well." Kee placed his cup on the coffee table. "What's more impressive is your sense of style. Didn't expect"—he whirled his index finger in the air—"that from a country bumpkin."

Lance snorted. "Yeah. Kee's pulling your leg, man. Don't feel bad for living in a house decorated by your grandma." He yelped when Kee slapped the back of his head. "What?"

"I was serious, you numb nuts."

Malcolm grinned. "Thanks, man."

Lance's eyes widened in horror. "You actually like this shit? Lace and étagères and furniture that fits together?"

Kee took a sip of tea. "Yeah. Because I'm not a twenty-something college student sharing a studio apartment with three other people and living on ramen. I have standards."

Cross chuckled. "Didn't see your high standards in your room at the facility, man."

"Because I'd never let my enemy see the real me." Kee shook his head. "Taylor and Thoreau have enough power over us as it is. No need to bare my soul."

Raine cleared his throat. "What do you mean he has power over you? I thought you follow Thoreau's orders because you're loyal to him. Grateful for your second chance. At least that's what Thorne told me."

Thorne shifted uneasily on the sofa, shooting his team members quick glances. "I did. But we all have different reasons for obeying those orders." He was still amazed that Raine already knew what he was capable of and didn't judge him for his past.

Kee raised one eyebrow. "I'm in it for the money. Priest only knows life in the military. Nothing else to do for an army brat. And he's the one with the conscience." He pointed at

Bailey.

Bailey raised one eyebrow. "I'll take that as a compliment."

"It's not," Kee deadpanned. He either ignored or didn't see Lance staring at him wide-eyed and in shock. "And stop deluding yourself, commander. You remained in the program for us."

Thorne growled. "Whatever." Damn Kee was too perceptive.

"I toed the line because I had no desire to be decommissioned," Cross said around the cookie in his mouth. "Assassins who rebel against an order are disposed of in a permanent way. And I had to think of Aaron. I'm responsible for him, since our parents are gone."

Alan cleared his throat. "Bailey told us. I wonder . . ." He pursed his lips. "Doc was the first to change sides. Now there's you five. How many more might we be able to convince to switch sides?"

"Not sure." Thorne pressed a hand against his belly when it growled loudly. "Sorry. Been a while. And I'm afraid cucumber sandwiches won't sustain me for long."

Bailey laughed. "No problem. Malcolm has a pot of chili on the stove. Alan, I might know a couple of guys who'd be willing to join your cause. But contacting them will draw attention to the pride. And me."

Alan sighed. "Even more attention, you mean?"

Malcolm raised his hand. "Is putting yourself in danger the only chance to end this madness? Asking for a friend." He frowned at Bailey. "No, really. How would you contact them? Sounds like a sure way to die young. If you leave on a mission, I'll go with you."

Thorne didn't miss the fact Malcolm seemed more concerned for Bailey than the pride he'd sworn to protect. Was there something going on between them?

Raine leaned forward. "Bringing more assassins to our

side's a good start. But we have to think beyond your fanged friends and their makers. Don't get me wrong. I'm all for ending Thoreau and Taylor like the criminals they are. How are we supposed to handle the other riffraff? Thoreau has a lot of Council members and other officials in his pockets. They support him. We can't kill every one of them."

Thorne frowned. "Good point, Red. Do you guys have a prison system? To a shifter, the thought of ending in a cage must be worse than death. Thoreau's a flyer, too. Prison would be hell for him. For the others as well."

Alan's eyes hardened. "Exactly. I second Thorne's suggestion. For a different reason."

Cross snorted. "Let me guess. You want to torture Thoreau and his associates?"

Priest shrugged. "It's not as though the asshole hasn't ordered others be tortured. Eye for an eye. Do you have a prison?"

Alan shook his head. "Most alphas deal with their troublemakers the way they see fit. Of course, the Council sets rules for punishments. But they rarely check to see if the rules are being followed."

Kee sneered. "Can I ask what else your precious Council does day-in day-out aside from making laws nobody has to follow?"

"Well." Alan pursed his lips.

"We have a different system in Europe," Raine said. "There's one representative per species to keep the Council small and better able to make decisions. And we have a cross-border branch of police. In each pack, pride, and so on, one officer who's not under the alpha's but the Council's jurisdiction is responsible for reporting crimes and mistreatment of shifters by their leaders. They also report crimes against humans. They rotate their location every two years to prevent corruption."

Lance stared at him. "Please tell me someone used the chance to call it Shifterpol. 'Cause that would be so cool."

Raine blushed. "The name's SHIP."

Thorne grunted. "Sounds reasonable. Why don't you have a shifter police force in America?"

"I'd love to discuss that topic, but we have more pressing problems to solve." Xander marched into the room as though he owned it.

Well, he probably did, being alpha. Thorne's nose twitched when he detected the scent of soap and musk. Xander's white-blond hair was still wet, the top part tied back in a bun. He reminded Thorne of a certain sword-wielding warrior in a series Lance loved to watch. At least his expression was just as grim.

Xander grunted suddenly and rocked forward. "Asa!" Slender arms curled around his neck while long legs closed around his hips. The man peeking over Xander's shoulder was the cutest little thing Thorne had ever seen.

Asa's hair was a wild mix of blue, purple, and teal and artfully tousled. His eyes twinkled mischievously as he pressed a sloppy kiss to Xander's cheek. "Sorry we're late to the party. My mate got bad news, so I had to help him relax." Asa slid off Xander's back and slapped the alpha's ass.

While Thorne's men watched the alpha mate with shocked expressions, the pride members chuckled, obviously used to Asa's behavior. Lance raised his hand. "Can we talk about the fact that—" He was silenced by another of Kee's slaps.

"My man's preferences are not up for discussion. I don't want to know what floats your boat either." Asa snapped his fingers. "Mal, why don't you serve your guests some of the amazing chili I smell cooking?"

After Mal had jumped up and left for the kitchen, an amused Bailey trailing behind him, Asa took the seat Malcolm had vacated and patted the place beside him. "Babe."

The sofa creaked under Xander's added weight. He looked horribly tired, but when his gaze fell on Thorne and Raine, a soft smile curved his lips. "Congratulations on your mating. I think I forgot that earlier."

Thorne dipped his head. "Thanks. Your mate mentioned bad news?"

"You either reached Alpha Hollister or got another nasty call." Alan turned to Thorne. "We've been getting them for a month. Only the inner circle knows, since we didn't want to worry the other pride members."

Thorne leaned forward, placing his elbows on his knees. "Tell us."

Xander sighed. "It's a little of both, actually. As everyone in this room probably knows, Alpha Mabel Hollister leads a sounder two hours from Wildcat Hills."

"What's a sounder?" Cross asked.

Kee scratched his chin. "A group of hogs. You should know the term, since we observed them for over two weeks."

Cross frowned. "I call them groups, no matter what shifter species they are."

"Are you always politically incorrect?" Asa glared at Cross.

"I'm a fucking assassin. Political correctness has no place in my line of business."

Kee rolled his eyes. "Shut the fuck up, Cross, and let Xander speak."

Xander cleared his throat. "Mabel informed me she was attacked two nights ago by a group of women clad in black and armed to the teeth. No pun intended. Mabel's enforcers killed two of them and chased the others off, but they lost ten people during the fight. And as though that isn't bad enough . . . she accused me of sending these killers."

Raine gasped. "What? Why?" A shiver rocked through his body.

Thorne tightened his hold on him. He felt sick to his stomach hearing Xander's news. If he'd said something sooner . . . if he'd left note of the alpha's name during his escape from Pumpkin Creek . . .

What have I done?

Alan's growl interrupted his self-loathing. "She's not the first. Over the past weeks, we got calls from our allies all over Nebraska. Two alphas said the men and women attacking them had worn the sign of the Wildcat Hills pride. A white lion's head. Other alphas informed us about different emblems on the killers' brassards. Neville Kelter, a bear shifter, said he was attacked by men wearing the Pumpkin Creek coyote head."

Xander nodded. He pulled Asa against his side. "Zelda Jacobs is the alpha of a bison herd. She claims her neighbor sent men to kill her and her mate in their house. It's getting out of hand." He met Thorne's gaze. "I want you to tell me what you know concerning the different brassards. Now."

Raine turned in Thorne's embrace and placed his hand on his chest. "Obviously, Thoreau generates suspicion and tension between the species. Did you know about his plans?"

Thorne shook his head. "I had no idea. We were scheduled to launch an attack on Alpha Hollister, but nobody ordered us to switch brassards. We only ever wore the sign of the Council. Priest?"

His second-in-command looked furious. "Nope. Never heard of it. I hate to admit it, but Thoreau's a sneaky fucker. In a time where the species should stand together against a common enemy, he's antagonizing them. He's pushing you into a war with your neighbors and friends. And while you're busy battling these small fires, he can do whatever the fuck he wants."

Alan frowned. "But his goal is to rule over us. All he's done until now led us to believe he's working toward a majority in the Council so he can change the electoral law. How does a shifter war fit into his plan of world domination? He can't rule over dead shifters."

Thorne thought Alan had a point. "A war makes sense if he's actively trying to destroy the resistance. The attacked shifters in Nebraska . . . are they all part of the fight against Thoreau?"

Xander raised his eyebrows. "No. In fact, when I called our allies a couple of months ago to warn them and ask them for help, most of them brushed off my concerns. The attack on them doesn't make sense."

"Well, it causes mistrust and alienates you from your friends." Thorne drummed his fingers on his thigh, his thoughts racing. "Have you considered the possibility that Thoreau's plan isn't leadership?"

"What else would it be?" Malcolm came back carrying a tray filled with steaming bowls. Bailey held a huge basket filled with bread in one hand, spoons and napkins in the other. The two men placed the food on the coffee table. Malcolm waved at the repast. "Help yourself."

Bailey picked the last free chair and sat down with a bowl and a piece of bread.

Raine took two bowls and handed one to Thorne.

"Thanks, babe." Thorne accepted a spoon and napkin as well and tried the chili. As rich flavors burst on his tongue, he moaned happily. "Fuck, that's good."

Malcolm beamed. "It's an old family recipe." He picked up a bowl for himself and sat down on the floor, leaning against Bailey's legs.

The other men helped themselves to the food as well, and soon the only sounds in the room were soft hums, the scrape of spoons, and the crunch of bread.

"Really, though," Asa said after a while. He waved a piece of bread. "What's Thoreau's real agenda if it isn't leadership?"

Thorne looked at Bailey. "Maybe the men you mentioned, the ones who might switch sides, can shed some light on the matter. They might know what's going on with the brassards."

Bailey licked his spoon. "Worth a try. I'll ask Romeo for their last known location."

"Romeo?" Thorne shoved another bite of chili in his mouth. "Who's that?"

"Our hacker." Xander smiled. "He's still busy sorting through the data Vaughn and Finley stole from the lab. Romeo and his mate Jules are working fifteen hour shifts to tackle the load."

Kee hummed. "Lance and I are trained computer professionals. We can help."

"Excellent." Xander placed his empty bowl on the coffee table. "You can start right away. But I want each of you to team up with one of my guys."

"No problem." Kee grinned, showing his fangs. "Lance, eat up. We've got to show the baby hackers how it's done."

Lance pouted, clutching his half-empty bowl to his chest. "I haven't eaten decent food in ages. And I haven't slept since . . . I can't remember. I need more food, a shot of blood, and a nap."

"You can nap next year." Kee stood. "Take the bowl with you, lazy ass."

Glaring, Lance snatched a couple pieces of bread and added them to his bowl. After a second of hesitation, he snatched another full bowl of chili and held it close. "You're such a slave driver."

Xander chuckled. "I'll send someone with a blood bag for each of you. Jaxon, show them the way so they don't get lost."

The enforcer nodded and rose. "You need me on patrol tonight?"

"Yes, I'm sorry. Djimon is too tired to pull another double

shift."

Jaxon smiled weakly. "I'll text Viggo. He won't be pleased."

Alan stood and clapped him on the shoulder. "I'll take your shift. Go and cuddle your wildcat. If I have to spend another evening with my bickering sister, I'll stake myself." Keeping his hand on Jaxon's shoulder, he steered the deer shifter from the room.

Kee and Lance followed them.

Xander sighed and stretched. "We're all tired. More so after the awesome food. Thorne, was your leg taken care of?"

"Yeah, Bailey patched me up." It irked him that he'd had to accept the guy's help. But Raine had threatened to withhold the blood if his pride led to an infection.

"Good. Go to sleep. Mal and Bailey as well. I need you clear and rested tomorrow so we can discuss the next steps. We won't get closer to the truth behind Thoreau's behavior if we hole up in Wildcat Hills." Xander stood and pulled a sleepy-looking Asa to his feet. He lifted his slight mate and hoisted him over his shoulder.

Raine got up. "I'll take care of the dishes."

Bailey helped him collect the bowls and used napkins, and together they carried everything to the kitchen.

Thorne shook Xander's hand. "Thank you for giving my men and me a chance. We won't disappoint you." He felt as though he already had, though. Just thinking about the dead hog shifters . . .

"Don't." Xander squeezed his hand. "I know what you're thinking. You're a leader. Every good leader feels regret. Every good leader feels guilt. The way you deal with these feelings determines if you've got what it takes to be a great leader. Don't let them eat at you until you're bitter and full of self-hatred. Accept your past and try to better your future. And . . . accept the gift of love." Xander winked. "Raine is no saint. From all the men in the world, fate picked the one who'll understand you better than you understand yourself. He chose you. Trust his judgment." With these parting words, Xander left the room. He shouted a good night to Bailey and Raine, who Thorne heard working in the kitchen.

Malcolm cleared his throat. "I guess you're my guests for however long you're staying. Let me show you to a bedroom. Do you want a shower? I've still got blood bags from when Bailey lived with me if you need a snack."

Thorne eyed the doorway leading to the kitchen. It didn't sit right with him that Raine was alone with Bailey. The good doc wasn't a fan of Thorne and had probably lots of disgusting stories to share.

Malcolm bumped him with his shoulder. "He's safe with Bailey. You know that, right? I understand your worries. But from what I've heard, your man is an excellent Council agent. Wouldn't be too pleased with you questioning his skills."

"You're right. Show me the bathroom. Got any spare clothes for me? I need to burn this ridiculous garment." He tugged at the Christmas sweater. Thorne raised his voice. "Red, I'm gonna take a shower."

Malcolm chuckled as he led him upstairs. "I'll find something for you and Raine. Do you need pajamas, too?" He waggled his eyebrows. "Feel free to be as loud as you want, by the way. I won't be offended as long as you're not offended by the thought of me jerking off while you get off."

Thorne snarled. "I'm aware you can't turn off your advanced shifter hearing. But my mate's sounds of pleasure are mine alone. So I'd appreciate it if you shut the fuck up."

Malcolm raised his hands. "Fine. Spoilsport." He opened a door to the left and stepped back. "This guest room has an attached bathroom. Towels are under the sink. Soap and shampoo in the shower. Feel free to use whatever you need. I'll go and fetch clothes for you and Raine. They'll probably be too big on your man. Tomorrow we can ask Finley if he's got something that fits better. They should be roughly the same size."

"Thank you." Thorne meant it. Although he hated relying on others, the times where he only had to think of himself were over. Raine deserved better than a life on the run and living in constant fear of Thoreau's vengeance. For the first time in over two decades, Thorne could see himself living in one place. In a house. With the man he loved.

But first they had to kill the bad guys.

CHAPTER TWELVE

Raine put the last bowl in the dishwasher and closed the door. He pressed a couple of buttons and the machine whirred to life.

Bailey stood at the sink, washing the wood board Malcolm had used to cut the bread. "So . . . Thorne bit you."

Raine arched one eyebrow. He leaned his hip against the counter and crossed his arms over his chest. "I was wondering if you'd use the direct approach. Yes, he bit me. It felt better than I expected. I heard how London suffered when you snacked on him."

"Yes." He coughed. "I also bit Malcolm when I was close to starving. He . . . didn't . . . I hurt him." Guilt rang in his quietly uttered words.

Biting his lip, Raine sorted his thoughts. "Maybe you hurt Mal and London because you were so thirsty. Why were you starving, anyway?"

Bailey put the board on a dish towel beside the sink, dried his hands, and turned around. "Because I was trying to kill myself."

"Oh."

"Yeah." Bailey laughed harshly. He waved his hand in a dismissive gesture. "You don't have to say anything comforting. I'm fine now."

Raine took a deep breath. His instincts as an interrogator pushed him to dig deeper into Bailey's problems. Not to lend comfort, but to gain knowledge to use against Bailey later. Raine pushed against those urges. Bailey was no enemy.

"Cat got your tongue? Look, you don't have to coddle me because you think I'm suicidal. I'm not a danger to others—or to myself—anymore." Bailey pushed his hands in the pockets of his jeans. "I eat and drink regularly from the bags Xander provides. Malcom makes sure of it. He . . . worries too much about me."

"Guess the feeling's mutual." Raine pulled out a chair from the kitchen table and sat. "Got some tea?"

"Sure." Bailey filled the kettle and put it on the stove. "Malcolm's hoarding hundreds of flavors. What would you like?" He opened a cupboard, revealing neatly stacked boxes of tea.

"You know your way around Malcolm's kitchen. Something fruity would be nice. I prefer black tea, but I had planned to sleep sometime in the next hour."

Bailey chuckled as he picked a red box. He prepared the teapot with careful, deliberate movements. "I lived with him when I first came to Wildcat Hills. Malcolm convinced Xander to let me out of the root cellar, hence becoming responsible for me."

"You hurt him while trying to punish yourself." Raine watched Bailey's shoulders tense under his thick cream-colored sweater. "I understand guilt, Bailey. But he likes you." One didn't have to be a world-class spy to recognize the heat in Malcolm's gaze.

"Xander ordered me to move in with Jaxon and Viggo. I'd have done it anyway. I'm terrified of hurting him again. You should have seen the terror, the pain in his eyes when my teeth left his neck." Bailey filled the teapot with hot water from the kettle and placed it on the table. He added cups and sugar. "Anyway. You and Thorne . . . is it real?"

Raine noted how Bailey skirted the topic of Malcolm's feelings for him. "We're mates. Yes. I claimed him and I feel the bond." Raine smiled. "Damn, I was shocked when I scented him. Him. The enemy. Just my luck."

"Do you think you don't feel pain when he bites you because you're mates?"

Raine poured himself and Bailey a cup of tea. "Yes. Most shifter species bite their mates when they claim them. I was worried he wouldn't stop. I was afraid I was only a snack to him."

Bailey cleared his throat and closed his hands around the steaming cup. A blush spread over his face.

"I've since learned that feeding feels good from the assassin's perspective as well," Raine quipped. "Blood is more than a source of food, right?" He couldn't help teasing the other man.

Bailey was a good-looking guy. Tall and broad. Steel gray hair and eyes. Designer stubble. Malcolm's fascination with the doctor made sense. The feeling was obviously mutual. But based on Bailey's questions, Raine guessed Bailey's interest wasn't purely carnal. He was curious to know how an assassin recognized their mate.

"Although you don't get along, you should probably talk with Thorne. I can only give you my perspective. I have no idea what if feels like for a vamp to find their—"

"Tea party?" Malcolm clomped across the tiled kitchen floor and threw himself into a chair, making it rock back. "Can I join? What are you talking about?"

Bailey tensed up again. His fingers shook where they were wrapped around his cup. "Ahh . . . I . . ."

Raine got up, taking his cup with him. "Look, I'll turn in for the night. See if Thorne is done with his shower or join him if he's not. Good night." He had his own messed-up assassin to deal with. He felt for both men, but he didn't need to add Malcolm and Bailey's problems to his plate.

Malcolm raised his brows. "Sure. I guess you had a long day." Then he smirked. "I told your boo you don't have to keep it quiet, if you know what I mean." He pushed his tongue into his cheek.

"Pervert," Bailey muttered. "I'm surprised you didn't ask to join them."

When Raine growled, Malcolm raised his hands in surrender. "Hey. I might be promiscuous, but I'm too fond of my balls to ask a mated couple for a threesome. Mates never share." He turned his head and watched Bailey intensely. "Ever."

Bailey swallowed visibly.

Raine cleared his throat. The tension in the kitchen had become thick enough to cut with a knife. "Well, I'll see you tomorrow." He turned and hurried from the kitchen. But he wasn't fast enough not to hear Malcolm's next words.

"Want to stay? It's been a while since—"

"I'm tired," Bailey said quietly.

A chair scraped over the floor. Raine heard footsteps. A moment later, the front door opened and closed again. In the remaining silence, the only sound was a heavy sigh.

Shaking his head, Raine entered the first room at the top of the stairs and sniffed. Thorne's spicy scent hit him full force, but he didn't see him in the bedroom. He put down the teacup, sauntered toward the half-closed door to the left of the bed, and opened it wider with a poke of his finger. The sight that greeted him took his breath away.

Thorne stood at the sink brushing his teeth. Bare ass naked.

And what an ass it was. High and perfectly rounded. The last time they were naked together, Raine hadn't had the chance to admire Thorne's backside properly. His back was a work of art as well, the muscles clearly visible under his dark skin. Like his arms, neck, and the side of his head, Thorne's back was tattooed. An amazing underwater scene with a trident prominently placed in the middle spread from his shoulders to the small of his back.

"Like what you see?" Thorne asked around the toothbrush

in his mouth. He spat in the sink and ran the water.

"You're gorgeous." Raine stepped up behind Thorne, pressed his whole front against Thorne's back, and looped his arms around him. His hands met in the middle of Thorne's chest.

Thorne placed one hand over his and sighed. He closed his eyes briefly, and a smile spread over his face. Their gazes met in the mirror.

Raine kissed Thorne's shoulder and breathed in the clean scent of his skin. "Hmm." He pressed his groin against Thorne's ass. He hardened in his jeans. When Thorne tensed, Raine hummed and rubbed his peck. "I want to hold you. I'd never do anything you don't want. You know that, right?"

Thorne's chuckle sounded strained. "You're very perceptive. Damn spies. I'm not sure if I'll ever be able to—"

"Shh. That's absolutely fine. You're my mate. Whatever we do together will feel amazing. And I don't mind bottoming for the rest of our lives." He wasn't much of a top anyway. "We don't have to have anal sex if it doesn't feel good for you." He kissed a scar left of Thorne's shoulder blade. It was small and perfectly round. Raine wondered if it was from a bullet.

"Until last night, I hadn't had sex in ten years." Thorne whispered. "Didn't jerk off until the incident in the cell. Self-inflicted celibacy because . . . stuff happened." He swallowed audibly. "I've never talked about that part of my past with anyone. Not even my team."

Raine kissed along Thorne's neck. "Wanna tell me?"

"If you tell me what it is that you need but none of the escorts could give you."

Thorne sounded genuinely curious, though Raine guessed he also wanted to buy a couple more minutes.

"What no man was ever able to give me." Raine licked his lips. "You grabbed my hair. You forced me to submit. You know what I crave the most, love. The feeling of complete trust. I mean . . . I need to trust my partner because I want to . . . let go completely. I can only do that when I'm a hundred percent secure in my partner's presence."

Thorne frowned. "A hundred percent is . . . a lot of percents."

"All of them, basically." Raine laughed quietly. "So?"

"So." Thorne leaned back against Raine's body. "I stopped having sex after Taylor forced recruits who'd gone through the treatment to fuck those who hadn't."

Raine gasped. "Why would he force you to have sex? And . . . which group did you belong to?"

Thorne briefly closed his eyes. "Both, eventually. He wanted to see if the turned individuals were susceptible to human diseases, and whether or not the vampirism was transmittable. To be fair, most of us didn't object to a little fun."

"Well, you obviously did or you wouldn't have trouble . . ." Raine squeezed him harder.

Thorne groaned and rolled his head forward. He placed his hands on the sink. "I should've kept that can of worms securely shut. Can't believe I'm about to pile more shit on you after you accepted my murderous traits."

When Raine ghosted his lips over the bone frog on Thorne's shoulder, his mate startled. "I'll accept anything you want to tell me about yourself. That's what mates are for. If you fall, I'll catch you. And vice versa."

Thorne looked up and turned in his hold. He raised his hands and slid his fingers carefully through Raine's hair.

"Trust," Raine whispered.

"A single day and you turned me from an oyster into a babbling idiot revealing my sordid past." He tightened his hold on Raine's hair.

"Nah. You're more akin to a sea urchin. Prickly and deadly

beautiful."

Thorne snorted. "You were right. I had an infection. One of Taylor's men recruited me at the hospital. A couple of months earlier I'd been given a dishonorable discharge for . . . sexual misconduct. The guys on my team notified the commanding officer that they witnessed me having sex with a male prostitute while we were on a mission in South America."

Raine growled. "What the fuck? A team is supposed to have your back, not snitch on you!" He caressed Thorne's chest. "The infection you mentioned . . ."

Thorne licked his lips. "Yeah. After the discharge I fell into a deep hole of depression. I knew something was wrong with me but I didn't go to the doctor until I broke down in a grocery store. Woke up in the hospital. A doctor kept babbling that I had to take responsibility for my actions if I wanted to live despite being diagnosed . . . positive." Thorne tensed as though he expected Raine to pull away.

Instead, Raine pulled him close. "Oh babe."

Thorne leaned in and snorted against Raine's neck. "Babe? That's ridiculous."

"Shut up and let me hold you for a moment."

"And there you go, being romantic and shit. Gag."

Raine placed one hand on the back of Thorne's bald head and pressed his face against his neck. "Deep breaths. A mate's scent is supposed to soothe. You might be a killer and get away with being a cold bastard to most people. But you need this closeness." He sighed. "We both need it. You're my safe haven in a world full of people who'd condemn me for what I did in the line of duty. I want to be yours, too."

Thorne's answering hug was so tight Raine gasped for breath.

When Raine felt dampness against his neck, he closed his eyes and rocked them from side to side.

"I'm sick," Thorne muttered. "I'm turned on by blood. Last

night I orgasmed because I bit you and tasted your blood."

"Well . . ." He was a vampiric species.

Thorne leaned back and rubbed his hand over his face, brushing away the moisture. "I know what you think. But I was like that before I was turned. How do you think I caught that virus? I was reckless. Lost control of myself." He crossed his arms over his belly. "The chronic hepatitis had already damaged my liver when Taylor found me. I'm cured thanks to his chemical cocktail. I wouldn't have let you bite me otherwise. But what a sick twist of fate that my thirst for blood will always remind me of the weakness that caused me to fall into Taylor's clutches."

Raine took Thorne's hand and pulled him from the bathroom. "Bed. Now." He let Thorne stand beside the bed while he hurriedly undressed. "We're doing this."

Thorne blinked. "What . . . no! You have no idea . . ."

"Enlighten me. What do you need?" Raine had suppressed his own desires while he'd been undercover. He didn't need to hold back with his mate. "You never have to feel ashamed with me." He sat on the bed, one leg folded under his ass, and reached for Thorne.

Thorne groaned and squeezed his eyes closed. "Fine. I want to bite you and watch the blood run down your creamy pale skin. I want to slowly lick it off you and do it all over again." When he opened his eyes again, desperation gleamed in the dark orbs. He licked his lips.

"We're a good match, since your bite turns me on. Shifter here. We bite and receive bites." Raine wriggled his fingers. "I'm not squeamish when it comes to blood either. Let's do this before I take a shower."

Thorne didn't seem convinced. Though he linked his fingers with Raine's, he resisted when Raine tried to pull him onto the bed.

"Wanna role-play?" Raine winked. "You caught me spying

on you. Now you have to tie me up and interrogate me until I tell you my secrets." Why not combine their kinks and double the fun?

Thorne laughed. "Red . . . you're unbelievable."

"Unbelievably irresistible?" Grinning, Raine leaned back. Predictably, Thorne followed him down and blanketed Raine's body with his own. When their naked skin touched, Raine groaned. He quickly wrapped his legs around Thorne's waist.

"Yeah." Thorne ran his nose through the valley between Raine's pecs and kissed the base of his neck. He placed his hand on Raine's knee and slowly moved it up his leg to his hip. "Absolutely irresistible. From the moment I first scented and saw you." He lowered his voice to a thick rumble. "Your pale neck called to me."

Raine shivered in delight when he felt Thorne scrape his pointy teeth over his skin. He held onto Thorne's shoulders. A stab of disappointment hit him when Thorne moved away from his skin. But Thorne latched onto his nipple and sucked. "Fuck."

Thorne's lips left his peak with a wet sound. "Hands over your head. I don't need rope to restrain you. You'll be good and do as I ask."

"Yeah." Raine nodded and obeyed immediately, clutching the slatted headboard. He hoped he wouldn't break the thing. "I'll be good, but I'll not share my secrets." He laughed when Thorne raised one eyebrow.

"Tsk. You say that now." Keeping their gazes locked, Thorne hovered over his pec. He slowly lowered his head and scraped his teeth left and right of Raine's nipple.

Raine gasped at the slight sting. "That's it. I mean . . . oh please, don't torture me."

Thorne laughed. "You're a terrible role-player, Red."

"Punish me?"

Thorne laughed harder. But then he focused on the cut and the humor slid off his face.

Raine gazed down his chest and stared at the drops of blood welling up from the scratch Thorne had left. When the blood slowly tickled down his pec, Raine's breathing sped up. Thorne's pupils were blown wide in his dark eyes. He made that weird growly noise in the back of his throat Raine had come to connect to feeding. Red shimmered in Thorne's eyes. Gasping, Raine lifted his hands to cup Thorne's face. He was transfixed by the change.

Thorne snarled, showing his fangs. "What did I tell you about your hands?"

"Oops. Sorry." Raine quickly put them back to the headboard. "It's just . . . you're truly magnificent." His heart hammered in his chest. To his surprise, his dick flexed and his balls pulled up tight against his body. Squirming, Raine groaned. "Damn. I think I could come just from you looking at me like . . ."

"Like what?" One side of Thorne's lips quirked up into a rakish grin.

Raine huffed. "Like I'm a three-course meal."

"Oh, but you are a very fine three-course meal. And I think I'll start with dessert." Thorne slowly lowered his head and dragged the flat of his tongue over the trail of blood. "Hmm. Delicious."

"Better than the bagged stuff?" Raine tightened his hold on Thorne's hips, hissing when their hard cocks touched. Hard. *Thorne is hard for me.*

Thorne hummed and licked some more. "That's like comparing a steak to cardboard."

Raine grinned and stretched under Thorne's body, trying to get more friction on his over-sensitive dick. "More. *Please*!" He hissed when Thorne sliced his fangs over his other pec, leaving a deeper scratch this time that bled more heavily.

"Aww fuck."

"Too much?" Thorne sounded worried.

Raine laughed. "No. Feels good!" Especially Thorne's rough tongue moving over his skin to catch every last drop. "Go on. I can take it."

Thorne closed his lips over the cut and sucked on it. "You're amazing, Red." He kept repeating the same pattern over Raine's upper body until they were both slightly sticky with dried blood and sweat. All the while, Thorne flexed his hips in a lazy motion.

It put such delicious pressure on Raine's shaft that he was close to coming. He'd never experienced a more erotic moment in his life. "Need to come, babe." Thorne's deep chuckle sent a tingle through Raine's body. "Please." Raine turned his head, offering his neck to Thorne. "Let me provide for you. I'm yours."

"Are you sure, Red?" Thorne ghosted his lips over his neck. "Don't want to take too much. If I seriously hurt you . . . I couldn't live with myself."

"Thorne . . ." Although Raine wasn't bound, knowing Thorne was stronger and able to subdue him easily if he wanted to was such a thrill. Thorne could overpower him, drink from him, fuck him, and there was nothing Raine could do against it. But Thorne was his mate. Thorne would always look out for him and keep him safe. He'd never felt freer. "I trust you. You won't lose control."

Thorne's answering moan sounded tormented.

A second later, Raine felt his mate's teeth against his neck and his hand around both their dicks. Thorne jacked them off with an almost painfully tight grip. Then, oh so slowly, he sank his teeth into Raine's neck.

Raine was done. The delicious bite of pain on both his neck and cock pushed him off the cliff. He came with a harsh cry, his seed splattering over their bellies. Thorne grunted and tensed above him. His dick flexed against Raine's, and more spunk landed on Raine's belly and chest.

Raine lay shivering with aftershocks, panting for breath, his numb fingers still curled around the headboard. He gasped when Thorne slid his fangs from his neck and licked the wound with lazy strokes. Raine lowered his arms and wound them around his mate. He caressed Thorne's broad back and nape.

Thorne purred. "Damn." He peeled his fingers from their softening pricks and sank fully on top of Raine. "You fried my brain." He breathed against the side of Raine's face, the fast puffs tickling him.

Raine laughed, but that soon turned into a yawn. "You're one to talk. Sucked the energy right out of me."

"Red, I'd love to suck you, but I need time to recover. And sleep." He snuffled. "Maybe ask me again after a week-long nap," Thorne slurred, sounding halfway asleep.

Although Thorne was fucking heavy on top of him, Raine didn't want him anywhere else. He angled for one of the blankets and pulled it over their tangled bodies until it at least covered Thorne's legs and ass. Raine didn't want to chance Malcolm sneaking a peek inside their room and ogling his property.

Thorne sighed quietly. "Thanks, my love."

CHAPTER THIRTEEN

Thorne kept sneaking glances at his squirrely mate. He was at a total loss as to what had happened between last night and this morning. Raine hadn't batted an eye when Thorne had revealed one sordid detail of his past after the other. Each of them could have tanked their relationship. Instead, Raine had held and encouraged him.

After last night, Thorne had thought everything between them was roses and rainbows. When he'd woken alone and found Raine showered and dressed in the kitchen eating breakfast, he'd thought Raine had just been famished. But while an overly cheery Malcolm had flitted through the house decorating the shit out of every room like a whirlwind high on Christmas, Thorne had felt tension between him and his mate.

His team, ever perceptive, felt it too. Priest wore his usual scowl. Cross had his please-can-I-ask-a-question face. Lance's glance flicked back and forth between Raine and Thorne like a kid afraid his parents were having a fight. He'd also plundered the plate of cookies in the middle of the huge table. And Kee . . . Kee was cleaning under his nails with one of Priest's knives.

Raine cleared his throat and looked pointedly at Kee.

Kee stared back unblinking. Thorne expected him to shrug off Raine's disapproval or at least refer to Thorne. Instead, Kee calmly flipped the knife, caught it at the blade, and handed it back to Priest.

Raine's chest puffed up. He threw a cookie that Kee caught

quickly.

"Conditioning my men, Red?" Thorne smirked. He had to admit, he was impressed.

"I call it fatherly advice."

"Dad, can I have more cookies?" Lance fluttered his lashes.

Raine laughed and relaxed visibly.

Thorne was completely focused on his beautiful mate. Raine's deep blue eyes sparkled with humor. And the pale winter light shining through the bank of windows gave his skin a creamy shine. His black luscious locks called for Thorne to brush his fingers through them. Or to grip them and smash their lips together.

A kick against his shin yanked his focus off Raine. Thorne snarled. "Something you want to say, Priest?"

"Commander, I see you're happy with your man, but can you please not eye-fuck him constantly?"

"The jealousy's leaking from your gaze," Cross quipped. "Because everyone around you is hooking up and you're not getting any."

Priest lifted his hands palms up and gazed around the table. "Who's hooking up aside from the commander and the com-mate?"

Thorne's team and Raine were alone in Xander's office slash conference room slash mission planning room. But the alpha and his enforcers would join them in a couple of minutes.

Cross leaned back, crossing his arms over his chest. "Well . . . I have a good feeling concerning me and McHottie the Sheriff. There was a definite sizzle in the air yesterday."

"He'll sizzle you with his stun gun if you keep molesting him," Kee muttered. "Moron."

Cross glared at the interruption. "There's also this guy." He pointed at Kee. "And you can't tell me you didn't notice the sparks between Doc Conscience and McRedhead."

Kee's eyebrows arched. "What the fuck are you—"

Lance coughed, spitting cookie crumbles over the table. "Kee hasn't hooked up with anyone." He punched his chest, probably trying to dislodge more cookie pieces that had gone down the wrong pipe. Lance shot a sharp look toward Kee. "Right? Kee? One of them cats caught your eye or something? Who do I have to slice to ribbons?"

Kee scratched his eyebrow. "Lance . . . tone it down."

"Oh. My Gawd." Lance jumped up, his chair tipping backward in his haste. "Tell me you didn't! When? We were together all the time after dinner at Mal's. Well . . . until a prim cutie dragged you off to show you his latest gadgets. And I know you didn't fuck him, because Jules is mated."

"Why do you care where Kee dips his wick?" Raine asked.

Moans and groans sounded around the table. Thorne palmed his face. "My mate . . ."

Kee's voice was low and calm as he stood slowly. "We're close to a war. I'm tired and overworked. Last night was the first time I caught three hours of uninterrupted sleep after two days of crawling through damp woods in search of our commander. And you think I've got nothing better to do than chase tail?"

Thorne didn't think it wise for Lance to stick out his lip in a pout. He gripped Raine's wrist and squeezed to keep him from meddling. Whatever he said would only make the situation worse. This storm between Lance and Kee had been brewing for months.

"Three hours of sleep? We left Jules and Romeo at about one in the morning and the alarm blared at six." Lance pointed his finger at Kee. "That's two hours you can't explain."

"Enough!" In an uncharacteristically impulsive move, Kee grabbed Lance by the neck and steered him toward the door. When Lance struggled against the hold, Kee threw the slenderer man over his shoulder and delivered a hard swat to his ass. "We're going to resolve this situation once and for all." Kee yanked the door open and shut it with a resounding bang behind them.

"Uh . . ." Raine blinked, looking around the remaining men in the room. "Did I say something wrong? Damn, everyone is so touchy this morning."

"Touchy?" Thorne turned to his mate, frowning. "We have something to settle as well. I need a clear head for our discussion with Xander, so we better get it over with." He stood, held out his hand, and wriggled his fingers. "Up."

Raine groaned and followed the command, though he didn't take Thorne's hand. He left the room through another door.

"Behave while I'm gone," Thorne warned Cross and Priest. He followed his mate into a room that came as a complete surprise. It was a sunroom with a worn but comfortable looking sofa, several wicker chairs, and a ton of plants stretching toward the glass roof or hanging down from the rafters. Thorne had never seen a room more beautiful.

Raine stepped up close to him. "Fine. What did you want to discuss?"

Thorne shifted his focus to the beauty in front of him. He placed his hands on Raine's shoulders and rubbed them. "You've been off this morning. Look . . ." He sighed deeply. "I'm not used to talking about feelings and shit. If I fucked up, you need to tell me or I can't fix it."

A blush spread over Raine's face. "Uh . . . well." He averted his gaze and bit his bottom lip. "It's not that you did anything wrong. I might have . . . read more into something than there is."

Thorne frowned. "Right. I have no idea what you're talking about. We started off being honest with each other and not mincing words. Let's keep it that way."

"Last night before you fell asleep you called me your love." Raine cupped his face. "I wasn't sure if you meant it or if you were tired or sexed up or whatever. I've been trying to get up the nerve to tell you that I love you. I know it's fast. And for a human it must seem crazy fast. However, I need you to know—"

Thorne yanked Raine close and caught his lips in a passionate kiss. Until now, he hadn't been aware how much he longed to hear these words. He hadn't heard them since his mother told him so when he was a kid. Thorne licked and nipped at Raine's lips until Raine opened for him. He tangled his tongue with Raine's, eager for his taste and the whimpers Raine fed him.

Thorne walked them backward until his legs hit the sofa. Reluctantly separating from Raine's plush lips, Thorne sank between the cushions and grabbed Raine's hip. He pulled him closer and pushed his nose into his mate's crotch. *Ah, yes.* His nose had picked up the subtle scent of beginning arousal.

Raine gasped, placing both hands on his shoulders and shoving lightly. "We can't! Your *team's* in the next room. *Xander* will be here any minute."

"Don't care," Thorne mumbled against the hardening ridge behind Raine's fly. He slowly popped the buttons while looking up at his mate. "I love you too, Red. Let me show you how much. I might be a touch rusty, so don't go shoving your prick down my throat right away."

"Romantic." Raine snorted. "As though I'd try choking a fanged guy with my dick. I'm quite fond of it."

"Me too." Thorne made quick work of Raine's pants, glad he hadn't bothered with underwear. As soon as Raine's dick was free, Thorne licked up the underside and curled his tongue around the head.

Raine hissed, placing one hand on the back of his head.

"Taste amazing, Red." Thorne also loved the heat and scent

of Raine's shaft. He felt the blood pulse under the silky skin. His mouth watered for another taste. Instead of giving in to his instincts, Thorne focused on his mate's passion. He wrapped one hand around Raine's cock while he cupped his smooth balls with the other, gently rolling them.

Raine panted above him. "Fuck yes. Baby?" He waited until Thorne looked up at him. "You don't have to watch your teeth with me." He winked.

Holy shit. Groaning, Thorne angled Raine's dick and took it as deep as he could manage. He sucked hard while using his hand where his mouth didn't reach. It took him a moment, but he developed a slow and easy rhythm up and down his mate's prick. Thorne closed his eyes, losing himself in the primal demonstration of his feelings.

Thorne loved it when Raine ran a hand over his head and held the side of his face with the other. Such a tender gesture. He didn't remember anyone caressing him while he gave head.

How Raine managed not to thrust his hips, Thorne had no idea. If their roles had been reversed, he'd be fucking Raine's mouth by now. Still, his dominant side as well as the sex-apprehensive part of his brain appreciated it.

"So good, Thorne. Fuck, I love watching your lips stretched around my cock. You look so hot. So in control. *So* fucking strong." Raine squeezed his nape. He panted harshly. "I know if I'm not good for you, you can easily manhandle me onto the sofa and make me bleed for my insolence."

Thorne groaned around his mouthful. Damn, his mate was amazing at revving him up. However, this . . . right now . . . was for Raine. So Thorne sucked harder, pushed his mouth farther down, and gave Raine's balls a gentle squeeze. Then, oh so carefully when he pulled back, he scraped his fangs over Raine's dick.

Raine let out a guttural moan that had to be heard by

everyone in Xander's house.

Thorne didn't care. He was too focused on swallowing and savoring every last drop of spunk Raine shot down his throat. When he was done cleaning Raine with his tongue, he leaned back on the sofa and pulled Raine onto his lap.

Raine snuggled into his arms, his chest rising and falling rapidly.

Thorne kissed the sweaty hair plastered to his forehead. "Good?"

"Amazing. Love you."

"I—"

A fist banging loudly against the door startled them. While Raine scrambled off his lap hurriedly, Thorne tried to stabilize him.

"Don't come—" The door opened, and Xander got an eye full of Raine's naked ass. To make matters worse, Thorne's team stood behind him, peeking around the alpha's broad form. "Stop staring at my man!"

"Shit." Raine landed on the floor.

Thorne's eyes widened when Raine's half-naked body started . . . rippling? It wasn't the first time he'd seen a shifter change forms. After all these years, the whole process still fascinated him. Thorne soon realized Raine shouldn't have shifted with his shirt still on. While his open pants and his boots fell away during the change, the shirt expanded and ripped in several places. Still, the green fabric remained twisted around Raine's huge form.

"Damn, your mate's a fucking big bird." Cross's voice was full of wonder. He squeezed past Xander blocking the doorway.

Thorne agreed silently. Kneeling on the floor beside Raine, Thorne stretched his hands toward the struggling bird he couldn't name.

Rapid, earsplitting chirps left Raine's beak. He lashed out

with lethal-looking black talons that measured about three inches.

Priest whistled between his teeth. "Commander, your man's a harpy eagle. He looks stunning."

Thorne wasn't sure, since his mate was currently a bird, but Raine seemed to glare at Priest. Thorne took his knife and held it up. "Hold still. I'll slice the shirt off you." Glad when Raine obeyed, Thorne made quick work of the shirt and took a moment to admire the creature before him.

Raine, finally able to stand, spread enormous wings and flapped. He chirped again and lifted the three longer feathers at the back of his head in what appeared to be a threatening gesture.

"You're beautiful," Thorne whispered. The feathers on Raine's back and wings were slate black, his head gray with a black beak. His belly was white. Under watchful gray eyes, Thorne ran his fingertips lightly over one of Raine's wings.

Raine puffed up visibly and chirped again. He dipped his head.

"He stands at least three foot." Priest sat on the sofa. "Amazing. What's your wingspan, Raine?"

Raine stretched his wings again and started preening.

Thorne chuckled. "I'd say six and a half feet."

Xander cleared his throat. "Sorry for interrupting. We'll leave so Raine can change back. I guess you don't want us to see him naked more than we already have. Asa will bring you clothes."

Priest stood. "Fine. I'll grill him for more info later."

"Thanks, Alpha." Hearing the door close, Thorne sat cross-legged and kept petting his mate. He couldn't tear his gaze off him. "I bet your claws and beak are lethal, hm? Do you hunt in this form?"

Another ripple went through Raine. The change didn't take him longer than half a minute. "Sorry. Panic reaction.

Shifters aren't shy. I wasn't sure how *you* might react to others seeing me naked. Did the best thing I could to cover up." He laughed and brushed a hand through his tousled black hair.

Thorne tumbled Raine to the floor and moved over him. He caught his lips in a deep kiss. "If I ever see Cross staring at your naked ass again, I'll carve his eyes out with an ice cream scoop."

Raine grinned. "Vicious. I like it. We better stop before you get us in trouble again."

"Me? You better appreciate my romantic declaration of undying love if you want another blow job anytime soon." Thorne got up on his knees, arching an eyebrow when he noticed Raine was hard again.

Raine shrugged one shoulder. "Mated shifters have a high sex drive. Be prepared to give me a hand job under the conference table." He rolled to his feet gracefully and stretched. "Damn, letting my bird free was great."

Thorne stood. He decided not to address the hand job comment. "We can head into the woods after the meeting so you can spread your wings thoroughly."

"That would be great. Thanks." Raine kissed him slowly. "Maybe I'll find a tasty raccoon."

Thorne grimaced.

"What?" Raine laughed, rubbing one hand over his chest. "Big bad assassin can't stomach the thought of me eating raw raccoon in my harpy form?"

Thorne placed his forehead against Raine's. "I'll get used to it, Red. For you. Promise me one thing, though."

Raine lowered his voice to a whisper. "Everything."

"Thoreau and Taylor are dangerous. They'll do everything to win the war we're clearly headed toward. Whatever happens over the next few months, I want you to stay by my side. You're capable and strong. But I need you safe and protected. You're everything to me."

Raine met his gaze, his blue eyes bright and solemn. "I'm sure everyone living here and in Pumpkin Creek is afraid of losing someone they love. We're playing with high stakes, so consider myself glued to your side. Because I'll make sure nothing happens to you, either. You're my whole world."

Thorne smiled and sealed the deal with a kiss.

YOU MAY ALSO ENJOY THE FOLLOWING FROM EXTASY BOOKS INC:

Breaking Point
Liza Kay

Excerpt

"There's someone else. I met another guy."

Roman blinked. "You . . . what? Can you repeat that?"

Wayne met his gaze. "I didn't mean to blurt it out like that."

Roman's breath left him in a gurgle, and he fell into his chair. "How did you plan to tell me then?" His chest felt like Wayne had plunged a knife into it. "You're kidding, right? Low blood sugar or something is messing with your head."

"I'm not kidding. It's . . . it's over, Roman." Wayne lowered his gaze. His face pinked, bringing an unusual flush to his pale handsomeness.

"How . . . how long has this been going on?" Roman choked. "Are you sleeping with him?"

Wayne looked at him as though he was a bit daft. "Of course I've been sleeping with him, given your lack of interest." He had the audacity to look indignant.

Roman curled his hand into a fist and brought it hard onto the table. "My lack of . . . We don't have sex for a couple of months, and you think that's me giving you carte blanche to fuck around behind my back? What about our vows? Don't they mean anything to you? I . . . I love you." His voice broke on the last word. Tears prickled in his eyes.

It can't be over. Not like this. He doesn't mean it.

Wayne didn't meet his gaze. "But I'm not in love with you anymore. You're . . . not the man I married."

Roman rubbed his hand over his eyes. "What the fuck is that supposed to mean?" Was it possible for his heart to shrivel into a little raisin and die? Just a couple of minutes ago his life had been perfect. Orderly. Predictably boring. And now, everything was falling apart.

"Please. Look at you." Wayne waved his hand. "You've changed so much in the past seven years."

Looking down at himself, Roman frowned. "Care to enlighten me?"

"You've gained at least fifteen pounds. Then there are your clothes."

Roman brushed a hand down his argyle sweater vest, over the belly that proved his love for a good steak and a beer after work. He had a desk job and no time to exercise. His chair was good, but it didn't prevent his body from putting on weight. "It's normal to gain weight in a relationship. And I'm not a twenty-something college boy anymore. Of course I don't dress like a frat party." This couldn't be happening. Wayne was leaving him because his style sucked? Who was the man sitting opposite him driving over his heart with a steamroller?

Wayne groaned. "You work from home and wear slacks, a dress shirt, a tie, and one of those awful vests every day. You never loosen up."

Roman got up and snatched his wine glass from the table. "So you're leaving me for my missing sense of fashion? Is that it? You've got to be kidding me. And this vest was a Christmas present from you! If my style is so hideous, why did you encourage it?" He walked around the breakfast bar to the fridge, yanked it open, and refilled his glass to the brim. Look at me letting loose and being rebellious. Look at me getting shit-faced.

"I didn't want to hurt your feelings."

"Oh, that's rich." Roman took a big gulp of wine. "And telling me you've been fucking someone who doesn't own a single sweater vest is not supposed to hurt me?" It was Roman's turn not to recognize his spouse.

Wayne sighed and leaned back. "I just . . . we've been developing in different directions. I want something else. Someone else. I want to go out with a guy who doesn't look twice as old as me although we're both thirty-five."

Roman's hand trembled. Wine sloshed over the rim and dripped down his hand onto the kitchen floor. "How old is he?" He sniffed. His nose prickled, promising a flood of ugly snot to accompany the tears lurking in the corner of his eyes. They were just waiting for him to open the gates.

Wayne looked guilty for a second, but he quickly schooled his expression. "Twenty."

Roman let out an unhappy, desperate laugh. "Aren't you a little too young for a midlife crisis?"

"Don't insult me just because you're mad." Wayne stood and grabbed his briefcase. "I'll contact my lawyer, Roman."

Fuck the steamroller. Wayne was about to flush their future down the toilet with a finality that twisted the knife in Roman's chest.

"I want a divorce."

Divorce. Roman lost the fight against his tears. He angrily brushed them away, but the harder he tried, the more they ran down his cheeks. A sob broke free of his throat. He choked it back, swallowed, and leaned against the cupboards for balance. "You . . . you won't even consider marriage counseling? You want to throw it all away? Our shared lives, our dreams for the future? You said I do," he whispered. "You said it, and I trusted that you meant forever."

Wayne shook his head. "Counseling? I'm telling you that I'm fucking another guy and you talk about our dreams? Our vows? People change, Roman. I have dreams for my future, but they haven't included you for some time now." He took a deep breath, then focused on Roman. "You probably don't believe me, but I'm sorry. This has been eating at me for a while, and I'm glad it's out in the open now."

Roman threw the half-full glass onto the floor. The sharp sound of breaking glass sounded overly loud in the quiet distance festering between them like cancer. "Am I supposed to feel sorry for you now, asshole? You're breaking my heart without giving me the slightest inkling that something might be wrong between us. You won't even give me a chance to make it right. You cheat on me. And you have the guts to stand here and tell me this is hurting you as much as me?"

Wayne's throat worked as he swallowed. He lifted his hands and took a step back. "Roman." Wayne stood two inches shorter than Roman and was a skinny slip of a man. But never had Roman done anything to make Wayne believe he'd raise a hand against him. Roman would never do that. Not even with the shards of his failed marriage lying at his feet. A marriage he'd thought would last forever.

"Get out of this house! Out of my house!" Roman sobbed and slid down the cupboard until his ass landed in a sad puddle of white wine. He didn't feel the moisture soaking into his pants when Wayne turned and walked out of the kitchen. Out of their life. He wouldn't have felt it if he'd planted his unattractive big ass in one of the shards. Roman felt numb. He hugged his thighs against his chest. Wailing, he let his head fall on his knees.

About the Author

Liza grew up in a tiny village in Germany, the kind where you know everybody and everybody knows you. She migrated to a bigger town to attend college, although her parents often wonder if she really moved out. Now, with a degree in her pocket, she's perfectly capable of working as a librarian. Never one to do what's expected of her, Liza currently browses different branches of employment.

She started writing in college when she found herself unable to ignore the guys living in her head any longer, and to distract herself from the stifling, non-fiction stuff taught in class. Liza is really fond of the dudes whispering in her mind—no matter if handsome or flawed, big or small, sulky or easy-going. They all deserve love and their HEAs.

When she's not writing, you can find her curled up with a good book and a cup of tea, a cat in her lap, or a camera at the ready.

You can contact her at onelizakay@gmail.com
Or visit her blog at https://onelizakay.wordpress.com/

www.ingramcontent.com/pod-product-compliance
Lightning Source LLC
LaVergne TN
LVHW020631100826
845148LV00012B/2135

* 9 7 8 1 4 8 7 4 3 2 6 4 5 *